Number sixteen in the hard-hitting Mayflower series of the doctor who lived by the only law the West would obey: the bloody law of the gun.

Jubal Cade 16

# MOURNING IS RED

Also by Charles R. Pike in Mayflower Books

THE KILLING TRAIL
DOUBLE CROSS
THE HUNGRY GUN
KILLER SILVER
VENGEANCE HUNT
THE BURNING MAN
THE GOLDEN DEAD
DEATH WEARS GREY
DAYS OF BLOOD
THE KILLING GROUND
BRAND OF VENGEANCE
BOUNTY ROAD
ASHES AND BLOOD
THE DEATH PIT
ANGEL OF DEATH

*Charles R. Pike*

# Mourning Is Red

A MAYFLOWER BOOK

GRANADA
London Toronto Sydney New York

Published by Granada Publishing Limited
in 1981

ISBN 0 583 13175 1

A Granada Paperback Original
Copyright © Charles R. Pike 1981

Granada Publishing Limited
Frogmore, St Albans, Herts AL2 2NF
and
3 Upper James Street, London W1R 4BP
866 United Nations Plaza, New York, NY 10017, USA
117 York Street, Sydney, NSW 2000, Australia
100 Skyway Avenue, Rexdale, Ontario, M9W 3A6, Canada
PO Box 84165, Greenside, 2034 Johannesburg, South Africa
61 Beach Road, Auckland, New Zealand

Set, printed and bound in Great Britain by
Cox & Wyman Ltd, Reading
Set in Intertype Plantin

This book is sold subject to the condition that it shall not, by way of trade or otherwise, be lent, re-sold, hired out or otherwise circulated without the publisher's prior consent in any form of binding or cover other than that in which it is published and without a similar condition including this condition being imposed on the subsequent purchaser.

Granada ®
Granada Publishing ®

# CHAPTER ONE

The afternoon sun filled the valley bottom with warm, golden light. To either side of the trail that followed the course of the narrow stream, the pines cast dark shadows over the late summer grass. Higher up the slopes, the topmost branches shone luxuriantly green, imparting a jade colour to the bare rock marking the rim of the twin spines of stone that formed the valley. The stream was crystal clear; silver rather than blue, the pebbled bottom fleet with the gliding shapes of trout. From amongst the trees a bluejay shrieked, the raucous cry answered by the melodious notes of an oriole.

The air was warm. Drowsy with the heat and the sweet scent of grass and pine sap.

The man lounging back against the seat of the wagon kept his hat tilted down over his eyes, shading them from the glare. A cigarette burned lazily in the corner of his mouth, the thin smoke drifting blue trails behind him. He let the two horses pick their own pace, the steady thudding of the hooves forming a counterpoint to the whisper of the stream and the trilling of the birds.

He was around thirty years old, a thick moustache adding authority to a weak mouth that smiled with lazy contentment as he headed west. A dark brown coat was slung over the backboard, and the man's vest was unbuttoned, his shirt sleeves rolled up to expose forearms corded with muscle. Like a farmer's. His pants matched the coat and vest: cheap cloth that didn't fit well, billowing over the work boots planted against the forward rest. A gunbelt spanned his waist, the holster tugged round to the left hip so that the butt of the Colt .45 jutted forward. A Winchester carbine in .44-40 calibre was propped beside him.

His eyes were halfway closed, the lids slack and threatening to shut completely as the warmth and the whisky he had drunk dulled his senses.

His name was Gil Last, and he was heading home from Gillard after buying supplies for his homestead up on the Wind River.

After spending three hours in the White Cow saloon.

He shouldn't, he knew, have done that. It was hard enough keeping the 'stead in supplies and his stock fed. Especially with a baby due. But hell! it was a month since he'd even seen another face apart from Jane's; and longer since his last drink. And a man was entitled to unwind a bit, wasn't he? After working like a goddam slave to get the spread in order. After spending the whole summer fencing range and building water traps to ensure a constant supply of fresh drinking water. After all that a man was entitled to ease up for a spell.

The cigarette burned down to the nub and scorched his lip. He spat it out. Carefully: onto the platform of the wagon where he could grind it out under his boot without risking a fire.

He reached inside his vest for fresh makings, thumbing tobacco and rolling paper with unconscious skill. The thin tube went into his mouth and he struck a match absently against his boot. Inhaled the smoke and dropped the spent match alongside the earlier cigarette. Then he reached for the bottle nestled in the folds of his coat. Drew the cork with his teeth and took a long swallow. The whisky hit the back of his throat and mingled with the smoke: he began to cough, his eyes watering.

While the coughing fit went on the two horses continued their steady plodding. They were long accustomed to the route and Last held the reins loose. He choked on the mixture of alcohol and smoke, reaching inside his pants for a handkerchief.

He was wiping his streaming eyes when the animals halted.

He thought, at first, that some natural obstacle had fallen across his path. And dragged the reins tight and set the brake while he cleared his eyes and mouth of the phlegm.

Then he folded the handkerchief neatly and shoved it back

inside his pants. Blinked a few times and saw the obstruction.

It was a man.

He was around six feet tall because his chest came level with the drooping head of the horse he held. He wore a black hat with a flat brim and a silver band around the crown. His shirt was a dirty white, open at the neck, and covered with a vest that looked oddly bulky. It appeared to be a mixture of cloth and metal. As though a chicken wire fence was woven into the material. It was buttoned tight, despite the heat, so that it fastened high about his neck and low down over his flat belly. He wore black pants with little silver conchos running down the outside seams, and a matching gunbelt with a holster tied down on the right thigh. The holster was empty.

The gun was in the man's hand. A Colt's Frontier model. The hammer was cocked and the ugly hole of the barrel was pointed at Gil Last's face.

'Get down.' His voice was smooth as the long brown hair hanging from under his hat. 'Slow. Without trying for that Winchester.'

Gil Last did as he was told. He got down from the wagon after wrapping the reins around the brake lever. Then he adjusted his hat, suddenly aware that the man was positioned so that the sun shone from behind him; into Gil's eyes.

'What you want?' he asked. 'I got no money. Only supplies. Sides of bacon. Flour. Salt. Nails. That kinda thing.'

'I want you.' The gunman smiled and holstered his pistol. 'That's all. Just you.'

He let go the harness and stepped sideways, pacing out towards the stream. The grass was firm there, springy and rich, hanging over the shallow bank to tumble fronds into the water.

'Why?' asked Gil Last. 'I don't understand.'

'You don't need to.' The gunman went on smiling his lazy grin. 'All you need to know is I'm here.'

Fear dispersed the fumes of whisky clogging Last's mind like the breeze that blew down the valley, lifting the gnats away from the water. He spat his cigarette into the stream. It made a tiny sizzling sound: like a dying gnat. Then the butt floated away through the shallows.

'Wain sent you.' Last's voice held a ring of finality. 'I won't go easy.'

'I work for Wain,' said the gunman, still smiling, 'but this one's for me. No one else.'

He lifted his arms out to either side, pale eyes studying Last's gun rig.

'You use cross draw? Or that just for ridin'?'

'Riding.' Last felt the palms of his hands get sweaty, and blinked as a salty tear dribbled down his nose. 'I wear it right side, otherwise.'

'Thought so,' nodded the gunman. 'Best hike it round, then. I don't like to kill a man without givin' him a chance.'

Last swallowed hard, curiosity fighting the sick pit of fear curdling low down in the pit of his belly. He stared at the man's face and saw that there was no other way to handle it. He swung his holster round to his right hip and fastened the thongs about his leg.

'Check the load,' said the gunman. 'I like to do things fair.'

Gil Last checked the load: the Colt was primed on five chambers, like always.

'I ain't no gunfighter,' he said. 'This is murder.'

The gunman laughed. 'I ain't drawn on you yet. I'll not draw before you got your pistol out. I can't do it fairer.'

'Christ Jesus!' Panic tore the remnants of the day's drinking from Last's mind. 'You're fuckin' crazy.'

He snatched the Colt clear of the holster. Thumbed the hammer back. Lined the muzzle on the man's chest.

Squeezed the trigger.

The Colt bucked in his hand. Powder smoke drifted across the stream.

Flecks of material burst from the gunman's vest where Last's bullet hit. The man staggered back.

And laughed and drew his own Colt. And shot Gil Last in the belly.

Gil screamed as the suction of agony tore through his entrails. He felt the bullet go in through the soft flesh of his stomach. Felt it rip through the muscle beneath and create a whirlwind of pain deep inside him. By the time it had ruptured a kidney and opened a fist-sized hole in his back, he was unconscious. Sprawled on the grass with a steady pulsing of blood channelling into the stream.

The water got darker where the blood fell in, then cleared as the current took it away. A brace of trout rose up to investigate the nourishment provided by the flies clustering over the blood. The bluejay screamed again and the gunsmoke drifted clear.

The gunman looked down at the body of Gil Last. The front of the homesteader's shirt was bright with blood, and from the back there pulsed a steady welling of darker crimson. He was on his side, curled up in a foetal ball, as if the concentration of his body might stem the outflowing of his life.

The gunman spun the cylinder of his Colt to work the spent cartridge over the ejection rod. He thumbed the spent shell clear. Thumbed a fresh load into the gun.

Then he laughed and went back to his horse.

Gil Last lay down in the grass and tasted the salt of his own blood. He could feel the pain deep down inside him like a shovel churning through his entrails. The blood in his mouth was almost welcome: it tasted fresh; fresher than the bile clogging his throat. Fresher than the dank, dark, stinking pit of sickness that roiled in his belly.

He pushed over onto his stomach and began to crawl towards the stream. Something was fazing his sight, but he could hear the gurgling of the water. Could almost taste the sweet, cool liquid. And at that moment of his dying he wanted nothing more than that coolness in his mouth. That sweet taste on his lips. Washing away the blood and the pain and the darkness.

Slowly, painfully, he inched over to the stream and let his face fall into the water.

He gulped down a few mouthfuls, then panicked as the liquid filled his nostrils and throat.

He fought clear, drawing back with great heaving gasps wracking his chest so that the twin wounds in his belly and back pumped fresh blood out from the holes. He spat water and blood and curled back into the comforting circle of his own body.

The two horses hitched to the wagon turned their heads towards the disturbance, then went back to cropping the rich grass, oblivious of the writhing body of their owner. They went on cropping until the sun faded behind the ridge to the west and the valley got cool. Then they lifted their heads and waited, tucking fretful hooves against the grass.

Twilight settled over the valley while the upper rimrock stayed brightly lit. The shadows crept up from the bottom lands to meet the shadows of the pine trees, creating a deep pool of darkness with the silver of the stream at its centre.

That and the dark shape of the wagon and the horses. And beside that shape a second: an indistinct shape that moved slowly – painfully – towards the larger bulk of darkness.

Gil Last moved on elbows and knees. Every so often he halted to press a hand against his bleeding belly. When he did, the hand came away slippery with blood. He reached the wagon and halted, resting flat on his face, sucking on the grass; too weak to move farther.

He heard a sound and tried to turn his head. The effort was too much for him, so he let his face fall back against the cooling grass and listened to the earth-born drum of hooves against the ground.

The sound got louder and closer. Then it stopped. There was the double thud of boots striking soil, a soft hiss of breath. Then Gil felt hands on his body and tried to speak. Tried to say, 'Help me.'

A voice that seemed to come from a long way distant said something that sounded like, 'Hold on.' And he felt himself turned gently over, tasted cool water on his face and lips. He tried to suck the moisture in, but the voice said, 'No.' And the hands took the canteen away.

Then, distant as a dream forgotten in the morning, there was the movement of hands on his body. Stripping his clothing from him.

He felt something cool touch his belly. Become hot. Felt the same alternation of ease and anguish wash over his back. He screamed, and the voice said, 'Easy. I'm doing what I can.'

Something pressed against the wounds. Wound over his ribs. Then he felt his shirt and vest and coat fastened tight around his body. Felt himself lifted and set back on the wagon. In the back, resting over the tarpaulin-covered supplies. For an instant, outlined against the star-filled sky and the overlay of bright-sparking pain, he saw a lean face with deep-set eyes and a short-cropped stubble of black hair outlined beneath the rim of an incongruous grey derby. He blinked, staring at the grey suit, cut English style, the chain of a Hunter fob-watch spanning the vest.

Then he closed his eyes and let the man pour something into his mouth.

It tasted bitter, and for a while he coughed, trying to spit it out. But the man held him tight and forced him to swallow the brew. Amazingly, it seemed to ease his pain, bringing a degree of clarity to his mind.

'Who are you?' he asked.

'Jubal Cade.' The voice was deep and firm and reassuring. 'I'm a doctor.'

'There ain't no doctor in Gillard,' mumbled Last. 'Not by that name.'

'I'm not from Gillard,' said Jubal. 'Where you from?'

'Up the valley. The horses know the way.' Last felt oddly dreamy. He wondered if Wain had sent someone to finish the killing. Then decided not: it made no sense to poison him after he had been gut shot. 'My name's Last. Gil Last. I got a spread up on the Wind River.'

'I'll take you home,' said Jubal. 'You got someone there can look after you?'

'My wife.' Last's voice was a throaty mumble. 'Don't hurt her, though.'

'Why should I?' Jubal asked.

'You'd not be the first,' mumbled the homesteader.

'Take it easy.' Jubal hitched his pony to the wagon and climbed onto the seat. 'Or you'll be the last, Gil.'

## CHAPTER TWO

Jubal allowed the horses to make their own pace. It was the only way he was likely to find the homestead, and the only way the man in the back of the wagon was likely to get there alive. He had done what he could for Last: cleaned the wounds and stemmed the immediate flow of blood; given the man a sleeping draught that should ease his pain and soften out the bumping of the ride. But without proper surgical attention, Last would go on bleeding internally and there was nothing Jubal could do along the darkening trail. Except take the man home as gently as possible and hope he lived long enough that his own body could use its regenerative powers to heal the deep gut wound.

Jubal doubted his attempt would be successful, but the training he had received in America and England still formed a hard core of purpose deep down in his mind. Once he had planned to practise medicine. Had studied hard enough to earn a scholarship that bought his way out of the Chicago orphanage to a training in London and Oxford. Had become a doctor – a skilled doctor – and won a bride. Then he had returned to America, filled with hopes and ambitions. With dreams. And the dreams had died in the blaze of gunfire and Jubal Cade had become what he now was: a vengeance hunter, seeking the man who had murdered his wife.*

He had killed men. Perhaps as many as he had healed, for he could use handgun and rifle as skilfully as he practised medicine. And a furious worm of rage churned deep inside him: a rage that protested the injustice of death that struck down the innocent while the killers lived.

It was that recognition of natural law, of natural justice, that

* *See the earlier JUBAL CADE books.*

had prompted him to tend Gil Last. That and the instinctive calling of his trade.

He had been drifting through the Nebraska territory for no better reason than a rumour heard in a Kansas saloon. One that said an outlaw gang was operating around Blazeville, led by a man with a scar on his face.

The man who killed Jubal's wife had a scar on his face. Put there by Jubal's bullet.

It was reason enough.

Until he found Gil Last, and found his desire to press on to Blazeville fighting with his ingrained training. With the instinct to help hurt people wherever and whenever he could.

He tugged a cheroot from his vest and lit the thin tube of black tobacco. Inhaled, puffing out a streamer of smoke. The taste reminded him that he hadn't eaten since the morning and he glanced over the wagon, wondering if the dying homesteader had any food on board. He saw the whisky bottle and chose to take a drink instead.

It went down fierce, burning his belly and throat, so that after the second swallow he decided he had had enough. It warmed him against the growing cold of the Nebraska night and gave a fast boost of energy, but he knew that he needed his senses clear to negotiate the trail. Especially if the man who had shot Gil Last was still around.

He flicked the reins to slap the leather over the horses' rumps, and reached across the seat to check the .30 calibre Spencer he had taken from his saddle.

The gun was old – a Civil War model – converted from carbine to rifle because he preferred the longer range and the familiarity of the lever action. It had been left him by his only friend from the orphanage: a bloody bequest of the War Between The States. Jubal kept it because it remained a tie with his past and because he knew how to use it. Was familiar with it, more than with any new long gun, such as the Winchester Last had.

He settled the Spencer across his knees and urged the horses into the upgrade flanking the northern edge of the valley.

The trail wound up through a series of terraces formed by the downspill of the hills. At first it was a straight trail that ran along a low slope flanked on both sides by grass. Then it got steeper and shaded by pine trees, the path going from soft dirt into hard rock. The last of the light faded away and the sky was filled up with stars, a pale crescent moon adding yellow light.

Under the trees of the upper slope the sky light was lost. For about one hour Jubal moved through total darkness, allowing the horses to find the way and only urging them on when they flagged. It was close on midnight before he reached the crest of the ridge.

Up there the stars shone clearer and the darkness of the trees faded under the moon's glow. He looked down on a wide valley with a timber-built house at the centre, two streams cutting through the rock to east and west to form a vee-shape that contained the building. On both sides, trees had been felled, exposing the flanks so that grass had taken over from the timber and slumbrous cattle grazed there. To the north and south there were dams, built up to control the water and channel it through the valley and the drop beyond. Without knowing much about ranching, Jubal guessed that Gil Last had made himself a fine spread.

If he lived to use it.

The windows either side of the cabin door spread a dull yellow glow over the stoop, combining with the moon's light to grant Jubal a clear view of the place. It was a single-storey building, a mixture of sun-baked sod and timber with a stone chimney running up the outside of one wall. It looked to hold maybe three rooms. Fifty feet away there was a privy, and behind the cabin a corral held a lean-to and a single, heavy-chested plough horse. Out in front someone had attempted a vegetable garden.

Jubal urged the tired horses down the slope, following the rutted trail that pointed directly towards the cabin's door. The wind shifted around and the plough horse snickered as the breeze carried the scent of the wagon team across the valley. Abruptly, a dog began to bark, its deep baying echoing through the stillness.

The door opened, illuminating the figure of a woman. She carried a scattergun across her chest.

She stepped away from the door, moving into the shadows of the porch, and said something to the dog. The baying ceased, dying away to a series of low growls that rasped like a drunk's snoring. Not quite loud enough to hide the double click of the shotgun's hammers going back. Jubal rode closer at an easy pace, anxious to avoid alarming the woman. Anxious to avoid the shotgun.

'Gil?' Her voice was soft, blurred by drowsiness. 'That you, Gil?'

'He's here, ma'am.' Jubal reined in too far out for the shotgun to be dangerous. 'He's bad hurt.'

'Oh, my God!' Panic replaced the anticipation and the dog's growling became a rasping snarl. 'Who are you?'

'Name's Cade. Jubal Cade.' He held the horses – anxious now to reach the fodder in the corral – on a tight rein. 'I found your husband back on the far side of the ridge. Someone shot him.'

She gasped something that might have been 'Gil', or 'God', Jubal couldn't tell, then called again.

'Come on in. Do it slow.'

Warily, Jubal let the horses move on.

'Where is he?' Her voice teetered between determination and hysteria. 'I don't see him.'

'In back,' murmured Jubal. 'I need to get him inside fast.'

'All right. But don't try anything. You make one wrong move an' you're dead.'

He braked the wagon close to the porch and climbed down slowly. The woman stepped back into the light and he saw that she was in her mid-twenties, black hair drawn back in two plaits from a face that would have been extremely pretty had it not been so tanned by sun and hardened by wind. Even so, she was still good-looking, her eyes large and wide-spaced, a blue so deep as to become almost violet, her nose tip-tilted above a generous mouth that exposed even white teeth that gnawed with worry at the lower lip. She wore a faded blue dress, opened at the neck where the buttons were too tight so that the beginning of her cleavage was exposed. Her breasts were full, swollen, the absence of underwear made obvious by the stiffening of the nipples.

The waist of the dress bulked out in a swelling mound: she was heavily pregnant.

She gasped again as Jubal climbed onto the wagon and lifted her husband down. She moved to help him, but then halted, lowering the shotgun to press a hand against her abdomen. Jubal saw that her time was near.

'I can handle him.' His build was deceptive. Little more than five feet six, and slim, he was wiry rather than muscular, but under the sober cut of his suit large bones supported a framework of solid muscle. 'Just call off the dog.'

The animal had its teeth bared now, black lips drawn back from long yellow fangs. The nostrils were distended and the ears flattened back along the skull. The whites of its eyes were exposed and the grey hair on its shoulders and spine was standing erect. It was a massive creature, looking like a cross between wolfhound and German shepherd. Its hindquarters and shoulders were bunched to propel it forwards. At Jubal's throat.

'Easy, Jim.' The woman settled the hammers of the scattergun down and reached to stroke the beast's neck. 'He's a friend.'

She moved towards Jubal, placing a hand on his arm and continuing to speak in the same soft voice.

'See, Jim? He's a friend. A friend. Let him by.' The animal's snarls subsided to growls, then died away. The woman went on speaking in the same calm voice: 'But if I give him the word, he'll kill you. Remember that.'

'I'm just trying to help,' grunted Jubal. 'That's all.'

She nodded and led the way inside the cabin. The dog

settled down on the porch, curled sideways so that it could check the valley and the interior of the homestead. Jubal stepped round it, keeping his distance from the jaws.

The woman swung the door closed, setting her shoulder against the heavy panel and dropping a thick slab of crossbar into place. The room ran the full length of the building, floored in scrubbed pine with rugs scattered over the wood. There was an open fire off against the chimneyed wall and a big, black kitchen range beside it, the smoke stack angled over to join the chimney. A table and two chairs and a big mahogany dresser occupied that end. The other held a horse-hair sofa and a wooden rocker. There was a low table carved from a single tree trunk with a preserves jar holding a few fading flowers on top. Facing Jubal were two doors. The woman opened one, leading the way into a bedroom where a carved pine bed held pride of place. It was covered with a rose-patterned spread that matched the curtains hiding the wooden shutters covering the single window. There was a dark-stained wardrobe and an over-stuffed armchair. The room smelled faintly of camphor.

The woman tugged down the bedspread, obviously finding it difficult to bend over.

Jubal lowered Gil Last gently onto the bed.

'I need hot water and clean cloth.' He tossed his derby onto the chair and peeled off his jacket. 'Can you handle that?'

The woman nodded. Jubal followed her out to the main room.

'I'm a doctor,' he said. 'I've patched him up as best I could, but I need to take a closer look. He was shot in the belly and I'm not sure what I can do. We may need to take him to a town, where they've got a doctor with full equipment.'

The woman's face went pale under the tan and her dark eyes got misty. 'There's no doctor in Gillard,' she murmured. 'The nearest proper doctor is in Blazeville.'

'How far?' asked Jubal. 'I was heading there.'

'Fifty miles.' The mistiness in her eyes coalesced into tears. 'Over rough country.'

Jubal shook his head: 'He won't make it. We'll do what we can here.'

He lifted the crossbar clear of the door and stepped past the dog. His pony snickered irritably, annoyed at being left hitched to the wagon. Jubal stroked the animal's muzzle and lifted his medical valise clear of the saddle. The bag was black and battered, the leather split in several places so that pale scars showed between the wrinkles. As an afterthought that was habitual, he lifted his Spencer from the wagon and carried that, too, inside. He left the door unlocked.

The woman was pumping water when he returned, her mouth set in a taut line as she humped the pans from pump to stove. Jubal took one from her, setting it beside the first on the big range. She smiled her gratitude, wiping a strand of raven hair clear of her tired eyes.

'How long?' Jubal indicated her belly.

'Eight months.' She sighed, leaning back against the chimney breast. 'Eight months, two weeks and three days.'

Jubal frowned. Suddenly his problems were doubled. Or trebled.

'Sit down,' he said, gently. 'I can do whatever has to be done. You take it easy.'

He helped her across the room and settled her on the sofa.

She asked: 'Who shot Gil?'

'I don't know.' Jubal shrugged, loosening the string tie and easing his collar apart. 'He said something about a man called Wain.'

'Jason.' The name came out like a curse. 'Father Wain, damn' him.'

Jubal was about to ask what she meant, but a groan from the bedroom caught his attention and he picked up his valise, telling the woman to rest.

He went into the bedroom and found Gil Last fighting out of the effects of the sleeping draught. He opened the valise and prepared another morphine concoction. Forced it down the man's throat. And then went back into the main room to wash his hands and fetch a kettle of boiling water. He stripped Last's clothes away and removed the bandages. Blood oozed sluggishly from both wounds, and from the exit hole in the homesteader's back there emanated a sour smell of poison. He cleansed the holes with hot water and medical preparations, scraping the tatters of flesh loose from the holes with a scalpel to avoid lead poisoning. Then he applied salve to both wounds and set fresh bandages back in place. The only thing left to him to do was to allow Last sleep, which he did with an injection of morphine directly into the vein of the homesteader's left arm. It used up most of his hard-won supply, but Last smiled and sighed and eased back against the sheets with his face set in a slack smile. Jubal covered him with as many blankets as he could find and went out to the main room.

The woman was sound asleep on the sofa. Jubal left her there and rummaged through the dresser in search of food. He located a side of bacon and a loaf of home-baked bread. Sliced two thick slabs of both and dropped them in a pan with the oil he found on a shelf. Then he went out and got the horses bedded down.

The dog – Jim – snarled at him once, then wandered round with him as he unloaded the wagon and took the horses into the corral. He forked hay into the feed trough and checked that the water bucket was full. Then he unsaddled his own pony and carried his gear inside the cabin. The woman was still asleep. He checked Gil Last and went to retrieve the burning food.

He was settled at the table, forking thick slabs of bacon into his mouth when the woman awoke.

She gasped and clutched her stomach. Jubal set down his fork and went over to the sofa. She had both hands pressed tight against her stomach, and her face was no longer tanned. Nor was it very pretty, because contractions stretched it into drawn-out lines and her lips were parted to allow a thin froth of bile to flow over her lower lip.

Jubal set a damp cloth against her forehead and his hands on her stomach. He felt the kicking of the child and knew that she did not have long to wait. Nor he: if Gil Last was going to live he would need constant attention. If Jane Last was to bear her baby successfully, she needed a trained midwife and better care than Jubal could offer in the lonely cabin.

He left the woman where she lay and went back into the bedroom.

His watch showed thirty minutes after five. The sky outside was getting light, and the first of the early birds were beginning to sing. He settled into the chair, swallowing the last of his first meal in around thirty hours, and went to sleep.

The smell of coffee boiling woke him and he stood up. His back and neck ached from the wagon ride and the night in the chair. He felt hungry again, and thirsty. He looked at Gil Last and saw the tell-tale traces of death on the man's face. The skin had taken on a waxen pallor and there was a blueness about the mouth. The eyes were tightly closed, but the nostrils were distended, stertorous in their fight for breath. The bandages were stained dark with blood.

Jubal changed the dressings and set fresh salve over the wounds. Then he went out into the main room. The woman was gone: he found her feeding scraps of bacon to the dog that sat up and whined for attention when he appeared. He ruffled its ears, surprised at the transition of hostility to friendship.

'Breakfast's cooking,' said Jane Last. 'How's Gil?'

'Not good.' Jubal shrugged. 'I've done all I can, but he's still bleeding. The bullet tore his gut up and I don't have the equipment to mend him properly. Maybe no one does.'

'Oh, God!' Jane clutched her stomach. 'What do we do?'

'What we can,' said Jubal. 'You'll need attention soon. You ever think about that?'

'Gil was going to take me into Gillard,' she answered. 'I thought to have the baby here, but it's been giving me such trouble he fixed on taking me in to Mary Wilson.'

'She the midwife?' Jubal asked.

The woman nodded. 'That's right. She's delivered most of the babies around here.'

'He should have got there sooner,' said Jubal; professionally. 'You'll need someone like that.'

'You're a doctor, aren't you?' Her face creased into lines of fear. 'Can't you handle it?'

'Not as well as a trained midwife.' Jubal shook his head. 'I got little experience with babies and you'll need care afterwards. I don't plan to stay around here.'

'God! You're a doctor, aren't you?' The woman's face lost some of its beauty as frustration and anger took hold. 'Don't you people take some kind of vow?'

'Yeah.' Recognition of the truth struck Jubal like a hand slapping over his face. 'Yeah, we do.'

'Then you got a duty to help us. Both of us. Don't you?'

'I was heading for Blazeville,' he said; confused. 'I got another duty. A personal one.'

'So you're ready to leave a dying man?' she asked. 'And leave a pregnant woman alone with her baby and a corpse?'

'No.' The word didn't come too slowly, though he regretted the commitment. 'I'll not leave you. You're right: I can't.'

'Thanks,' said Jane Last, and doubled over as fresh pain hit her. 'Thanks a lot.'

The dog barked, skirting around Jubal's legs as he helped the woman back inside the cabin. He set her down on the sofa and bathed her sweaty face before checking the distension of her stomach. The spasms were coming harder now, the movement of the baby's feet stronger against her distended belly. He left her there, a cool cloth laid over her forehead and the dog licking at her hand as he went to check her husband.

Gil Last was dead.

The pillow beneath his head was stained and thick with the flood of blood that had poured from his mouth. His nostrils were flecked with mucus and the sheets and blankets wrapped about his body were coloured a dark crimson. The writhings of his death agony had torn the bandages loose so that tatters of scarlet crimson hung down from the sides of the blood-stained bed.

Jubal went out past the unconscious woman and found a spade in the lean-to. He dug a shallow grave and carried Gil Last over to the hole. By then Jane had woken up again and followed him out. She tossed the first handful of dirt over her husband's face before slumping down with both hands bleeding tears through her clutching fingers as Jubal began to spade earth down over the corpse. He found two pieces of suitable timber in the lean-to and a knife in the kitchen. Carved *Gil Last* on the shortest piece and then nailed it to the longer section. Used the spade to hammer the make-shift cross into the turned soil, and stamped the hump flat.

Then he hitched the wagon horses up and made sure there was sufficient food for the plough animal.

While he worked, Jane Last sat staring at the grave with tears running down her cheeks to stain the material of her dress.

Jubal damped the fire inside the cabin and fetched enough bedding to make a comfortable nest in the wagon. He set a mattress over the bed and covered it with a blanket and a sheet, then set pillows and cushions around the edges. He remembered to pack clothing into the carpet-bag he found in the bedroom, then lifted the woman on board. Covered her with more blankets, and locked the tail-gate in place.

'The dog! Bring Jim,' she mumbled. 'I can't leave him.'

Jubal whistled, motioning at the wagon. The big dog yelped and ran forwards to launch his weight upwards onto the seat. Jubal fetched his own pony from the corral and hitched it behind. He set his saddle and bags on the seat. Stashed the Spencer close at hand, and climbed astride himself.

'How far to Gillard?' he asked. 'What kind of trail?'

'I can make it,' she said. 'It's about five hours.'

'Like I told your husband,' grunted Jubal, 'I hope they're not your last.'

# CHAPTER THREE

By day's light the trail was easier to follow, and he held the horses to as fast a pace as he thought safe for the woman. She remained reasonably comfortable in the back of the wagon, uncomplaining except when they crossed some particularly rough section of the ground.

The big dog appeared to suffer more discomfort, springing clear of the seat to bound alongside after the first slanting of the upgrade. Jubal left the animal to find its own way, concentrating on reaching the spot where he had found Gil Last. It was noon by the time he reached the second valley, and then he had to ask directions of Jane. She told him between gasps of pain, indicating that he should continue along the side of the stream until he reached the outspill, then turn west down the line of a low bluff, from which he would see the town. He digested her instructions and urged her to rest, to sleep if she was able. He was worried that the imminent birth of her child might be brought farther forward by the shock of her husband's death, anxious to find the midwife before that started.

He followed the stream and took the trail curving past the overspill of the bluff. As he rounded the final curve of the ridge he saw the land drop away in a gradual slope that culminated in the basin of an enormous valley. A broad, shallow river flowed down the centre, the banks dotted with cottonwood and thickets of aspen. A mile on there was the dark bulk of a growing township feeding smoke into the clear air. Jubal steered towards it, whistling for the big dog to follow.

Gillard was built along the north side of the river. It was a largish town for so lonely a section of country, the main street stretching several hundred yards, with side streets cut in at right angles. There was a bank and a marshal's office; a hotel and two saloons; an eating house and a spread of shops selling everything from guns to hair ribbons. Jubal followed the trail down until he hit mainstreet, then paused to ask the woman for directions to Mary Wilson's home.

It was a clapperboard frame house along a side street. Flowers grew behind a peeling picket fence, and an apple tree was fighting to survive in the centre of the garden. The woman who answered Jubal's knock looked like the tree.

She was anything upwards of fifty, her hair grey, dragged back in a tight bun that was fastened with pins and a black net. Deep-scored wrinkles creased over her face and her eyes were bright blue, suspicious as a bird's.

'What you want?' Her voice was sharp. 'That's Gil Last's wagon, ain't it?'

'Yeah.' Jubal nodded. 'His wife's in the back. Her time's come.'

'Where's Gil?' The old woman straightened up with the aid of a walking cane. 'How come he ain't with Jane?'

'He's dead,' said Jubal. 'I found him on the trail yesterday. He was gut shot. He died at home, so I brought his wife in to you.'

'Why?' Mary Wilson tapped her cane irritably on the polished stoop. 'I don't want no trouble.'

'Her time's come,' Jubal repeated. 'Her husband's dead and I couldn't leave her alone up there. She mentioned your name: so I brought her in.'

He felt the ugly pricklings of trouble stirring in his mind, and wished that he'd chosen another route to Blazeville. One that might have taken him clear of Gil Last.

He kept the doubts to himself, pointing at the wagon.

'Shall I bring her in?'

'Oh, goddamit, all I ever get is problems. If it aint one thing it's another. Jane ain't been nuthin' but trouble since the day she got born.' Mary Wilson fretted her stick against her high-button boots. 'Get her inside, son. Ain't no one else overly anxious to help her. Not around here, leastways.'

Jubal went back to the wagon and lowered the tailboard. Jane Last was awake again, clutching her stomach and moaning softly. He half-helped her, half-lifted her clear, and then half-carried her into the house. The big dog followed behind.

'I ain't havin' that monster round here,' snapped the midwife. 'An' I don't want that team hitched outside my fence. You get rid of the whole damn' thing.'

Jubal shrugged. 'What do I do with them? I'm just passing through.'

'I don't care.' The old woman helped Jane to a bed and began to unfasten her clothes. 'I tend pregnant women, not goddam dirty animals. You leave this poor girl with me, an' she'll be all right. You do what you want with those beasts out there.'

'I'll put them in the stable.' Jubal backed away, pleased to have the problem taken out of his hands. 'I'll ask them to tend the dog. Tell her that, will you?'

'Who pays?' demanded the old woman. 'Jane an' Gil never had a penny to rub together. Not the way he was buildin' things. Goddam fool.'

'I'll pay.' Jubal said it fast, eager to get away. 'I'll settle for one week.'

'She'll need longer if Gil's dead,' grunted the midwife. 'Need a whole goddam lifetime.'

Jubal didn't hear because he was already closing the door. He whistled up the dog and climbed back on the wagon, taking the horses up the side street and then angling round to enter main-street again and steer towards the livery he had seen.

It was set back towards the river, a tall building with windows opening out of the hay loft and wide double doors at the front. An old man with grey hair and gold-rimmed spectacles was chewing tobacco on a chair at the front. He spat a stream onto the ground as Jubal came up, and said, 'I don't take no dogs.'

'How much for the wagon and team?' Jubal asked. 'Fodder included.'

'Sixty cents a day.' The oldster cut a fresh wad and fed it inside his mouth. 'Week in advance.'

Jubal handed over one week's money plus ten dollars.

'Leave the dog with the horses. Keep him tied up.'

'That's Gil Last's dog, ain't it?' The old man mouthed a too-hard strand across the ground. 'I ain't sure I want nuthin' to do with Gil Last's dog.'

'You want the extra ten or not?' Jubal demanded. 'All you need do is keep the dog until Mrs Last has her baby.'

'Her baby?' The old man's face changed shape as it smiled. 'You mean ole Jason got a grandson? Where's Gil?'

'Dead,' Jubal said, repeating the story. 'I found him shot and took him home. He died there.'

'An' Jane's got the baby comin'?' mused the oldster. 'Here in town?'

'Like I told you,' grunted Jubal. 'You willing to take the dog, or not?'

'I guess.' The old man's creased face wrinkled even more. 'Where's Jane?'

'I left her with the midwife,' Jubal replied.

'Mary Wilson?' The stablehand chuckled. 'Sour-tongued ole biddy?'

'Yeah.' Jubal nodded, wondering why there was so much interest in the pregnant woman's location. 'That was her name.'

'Well.' The old man chuckled. 'Don't that beat all? I guess you're a stranger round here.'

'That's right,' nodded Jubal. 'And all I want to do is beat it out of here.'

'In that case, I'll take yore money.' A gnarled hand shot out faster than the bent body looked capable of moving. 'I'll take the dog an' throw in some advice fer free.'

Jubal watched the note folded inside the sweaty shirt, waiting. The old man chuckled some more, dribbling tobacco over his stubbled jaw.

'My advice is you quit Gillard fast as you can, mister. Ole Jason don't take kindly to folks helpin' the Lasts. Might be wise if you took yore pony right now, an' rode away. Far an' fast as you can.'

'Tomorrow.' Jubal shook his head. 'If I stepped into some family feud I don't want to know. All I did was help a shot man and a pregnant woman. I don't aim to stay around.'

'Your choice.' The stablehand shrugged. 'But don't say that Billy Judge didn't warn you.'

Jubal turned away, not interested in whatever local news the old man had to impart. He had done as much as his conscience as a doctor dictated: he had tried to save Gil Last's life and then buried the man; he had brought Jane Last to the midwife and spent his own money on her animals. His conscience was clear: he had done everything he could, and now he was free to ride on to Blazeville in search of Lee Kincaid. He had already made a wide detour that had lost him a night's sleep, so now that he was in a town he thought to catch up on that. And start fresh come morning.

He took his saddlebags and the medical valise and walked back into the centre of Gillard, heading for the hotel.

It was two floors high, with a massive board hung on the front, bearing the scarlet-lettered legend: *The St David Hotel. Travellers welcome.* The paint was faded and the wood was peeling, and bullet holes clustered inside the *o*'s. Two dying shrubs stood in fancy tubs either side of the door. Inside, there was a vestibule shuttered off from the main lobby by glass panels, one of which had been shattered and replaced by a sheet of oil cloth. The walls were covered in plush paper, all crimson and gold velour, and a matching carpet covered the floor. A second glass-fronted door opened into a restaurant, and a flight of carpeted stairs led up to the balcony overhanging the passageway leading to the ground floor rooms.

Jubal booked a room for the night and a bath in one hour. He checked his bags and the Spencer into his room and then went looking for a barber.

He found the place two blocks down. Got a shave and haircut, then returned to the hotel. He arranged for his suit and shirt to be cleaned and pressed and stretched out on the bed, trying not to think about Jane Last and her baby.

The knocking at the door woke him from sleep and he went to take his bath. He dozed off again in the tub, suddenly aware of the weariness filling his limbs. It had been a long, hard ride up from Kansas, his determination to find Mary's killer spurring him on to excesses of hardship that had denied him sleep and food for too long. He knew that he needed rest. Knew that he needed to harbour his energies for the confrontation he hoped to find. But at the same time found it difficult to allow that luxury to hold him away from his vengeful mission. This was the first time in two months he had spent time away from the trail; time to pause and luxuriate in a hot bath or a soft bed for more than a few hours at a time.

Weariness and guilt and hate combined.

Weariness won, and the hot water claimed him, taking him down into sleep that ended only when the windows were dark and the water cold. He rose from the scum of saddle dirt and sluiced his lean body with cold water. Then he towelled dry and reclaimed his clothes. His watch showed seven o'clock: he went down to dinner.

The dining room was mostly empty, and he ate a steak with hash greens and mashed potato, washed down with coffee. When he was finished he no longer felt sleepy, but knew that a night's rest in a comfortable stable would benefit his pony. He quit the hotel and went into the nearest saloon.

It was a place called the Gillard Empire. A one-room building with huts out back to sleep the girls and their clients. There was a long bar running down one side of the room, teak and rosewood combined under a scarring of boots and spurs. Two barmen were handling around thirty drinkers, half that number occupied with poker or keno. Jubal asked for a whisky and a beer.

The barkeep who took his order was young: not much over twenty, with thick brown hair slicked back under a spread of pomade that gave off the sour odour of dead violets. He lingered around, obviously plucking up the courage to ask a question.

By the time Jubal was on his second whisky he found the nerve to ask it.

'You the feller brought Jane Last in?'

Jubal nodded.

'You think you'll see her again?' The barkeep began to polish glasses with deceptive vigour. 'Before you leave town?'

'I doubt it.' Jubal downed his second whisky and topped the glass from the bottle the young man pushed towards him. 'I just did what anyone'd do. I ride on, come morning.'

'But Gil's dead, ain't he?' The barkeep's scrubbing got harder, the cloth brushing furiously around the rim of the glass. 'Like Billy Judge said.'

'He looked pretty dead when I shovelled the earth on his face,' grunted Jubal. 'Why?'

'Nothing.' The barkeep swallowed hard and the glass he was polishing shattered in his hand. 'Mostly gossip. Nothing else.'

'Yeah.' Jubal finished his drink and drained the last of the beer. 'Nothing else at all, so far as I'm concerned.'

He tossed some coins on the bar and quit the saloon. The night had turned chilly, so he folded the collar of his suit up around his ears and settled the grey derby tighter over his fresh-cropped head. The thought of a warm, soft bed was tempting, and he walked quickly back to the St David.

He slept soundly and in the morning he shaved in the hot water brought to his room, ate breakfast, and settled his bill. The sun was still climbing across the sky when he left. It was eight o'clock and Gillard was just beginning to wake up. There was a smell of cooking in the air, mingling with the chill coming down off the mountains. The street was cold, still except for the clopping of the few riders heading down main-street for the farms and ranches spread out beyond the town. Jubal hiked his saddlebags over his left shoulder and slung the Spencer over his right as he paced towards the stable.

There was a brazier lofting smoke into the air at the front

and pools of frosted tobacco spit around it, but no sign of Billy Judge. Jubal pushed through the door and shouted for the stablehand.

There was no answer, except the snicker of his own pony and the bark of Jane Last's dog.

He shrugged, squinting his eyes against the gloom of the stable. The sun was not yet high enough to filter illumination in through the narrow windows, so the whole long hut was wrapped in early morning twilight. He paced down the central aisle scanning the stalls on either side until he saw his horse.

The bay pony was in the cubicle next to Jane Last's two wagon horses, which were stabled in the end pen, one larger than the others so that it might contain animals accustomed to herding together.

The dog was whining on the end of a short rope between the horses.

Jubal grinned at the animal and slung his gear over the gate. He lifted the rope clear of the gate and stepped inside the pen. The bay set to shuffling as Jubal slung the saddle on its spine and lifted a knee into its belly so that it breathed in as he fastened the girth straps. He checked the stirrups and settled the bridle into the animal's mouth. Fastened his saddlebags in place and shunted the Spencer into the boot.

The dog went on whining as he turned the pony around and led it clear of the stall.

Then he slung his valise over the saddle horn.

And felt something hard and deadly ram against the small of his back.

It shoved him forwards so that he lost his balance and was forced to grab the swinging gate to stay upright. A voice said, 'You brought Jane Last into town. That right?'

Jubal groaned and said, 'Sure. She was pregnant. What else could I do?'

A second voice, thick with laughter, said, 'Leave her, feller. Ride away.'

'I was going to do that.' Jubal turned his head, but the

muzzle of the Winchester snapped against his jaw, twisting his answer back into the stall.

'That wasn't soon enough,' said the first voice. 'It was nine months too late.'

'I didn't know that,' Jubal said. 'All I want to do is get to Blazeville.'

'Tough.' The voice was hard, but slightly lisping. As though it wasn't sure of what it was doing. 'You just left it too late.'

Jubal began to ask why, but the butt of the rifle slammed against his back, landing between the shoulderblades. He groaned, his hands snapping clear of the fence as the blow slammed pain down his back. He fell onto his knees, and felt the rifle smash across the side of his head. He fought to stay upright, but someone kicked his legs from under him. He felt the rifle butt land again, and then there was nothing but pain.

There were feet that drummed against his back and sides as he rolled into a ball with his legs drawn up tight against his belly and his arms cushioned around his head. He rolled, moving under the blows so that the pain was spaced out and he was protecting as many vital points as he could. It was a technique he had learnt in the Chicago orphanage. One that he hoped would keep him alive in Gillard, Nebraska.

After a while the pain stopped and the kicking went away. He heard someone shout, 'What's going on?'

Then there was darkness and a sensation of movement.

He felt himself lifted and tied.

Someone called, 'That ain't right. He's too bad hurt.'

Then there was movement again and a blow that blanked out all the light.

## CHAPTER FOUR

There was pain.

Pain and hate.

He rested back against the cool grass of the trail, letting the moisture soak into his clothes and his skin so that it numbed the bruising of the beating. Let it soak through him until he was ready to open his eyes again and look at the world.

It was bright. A big pine tree spread shadow over his face and off to the side a cottonwood dappled light down over the trail. A thrush was trilling in the branches above him and an oriole was answering from down on the slope. The sun was slanting rays of light over his face and motes of dust spun in the air where the rays shone through the trees.

Jubal rolled over and spat blood. He checked his mouth, running his fingers over the broken edges of the front teeth. They were intact, so he checked his ribs: heavily bruised, but not broken. His arms and legs were in the same condition: savagely bruised by the kicking, but not permanently damaged.

He forced his body upright, blinking ashes of pain from his eyes as he tried to see clear.

The bay pony was hitched to a pine. The saddlebags were open and Jubal's gear strewn over the grass. He stumbled across to the horse, groaning as he stooped to retrieve his clothes. When he had the bags repacked he made a fast inventory: his medical valise was intact; his rifle was undamaged, several cartons of ammunition unopened. The only missing item was the $1,800 dollars that had been wrapped inside a shirt.

There was a note on his saddle. It read: *Dont cum back or we will kill yu.*

Anger overcame the aching of his bruised body and he felt

his facial skin draw taut as rage possessed him. He folded the note inside his vest and climbed awkwardly astride the pony. Turned its head back the way he had come. Back towards Gillard.

Evening was settling in as he entered the town again. He put the horse back in the stable and checked back into the hotel. The clerk saw his face and frowned. Jubal grinned an ugly smile and said, 'I got worse marks in other places.'

'Private, I guess.' The clerk handed him a room key. 'You look like you could use a doctor.'

'Physician heal thyself,' Jubal muttered. 'Trouble is, I can't reach all the bits that need it.'

'Mary Wilson is very good,' suggested the clerk. 'Knows how to massage the kinks out.'

Jubal was surprised: that kind of massage was not what he expected to find in a cattle town.

'I could send for her,' said the clerk. 'While you take a bath.'

'Thanks.' Jubal nodded and went up to his room and the hot tub.

When he climbed out, Mary Wilson was waiting for him, looking like she had taken control.

The curtains were pulled across the blinds and the bed was stripped down to its boards. There was a tub of hot water beside the bed and a pan of steaming wax on the washstand.

'Stretch out,' said the old lady. 'Ease back.'

Jubal did like he was told, giving himself up to her ministrations with a grateful sigh.

She was good: knew what she was doing. She kneaded his muscles with rough expertise that loosened the kinks and left him feeling supple again, the bruises forgotten. When she was finished she slapped his back and said, 'What happened?'

'Two cowboys jumped me in the stable,' he said. 'They grabbed me before I could do anything.'

'Be Jason Wain's men,' she said. 'Goddam outlaws, most of 'em.'

Jubal eased clear of the bed with a towel dropping from around his waist.

'Why?' he asked. 'Why do that?'

'You don't know?'

He shook his head, forgetting the loss of the towel.

'Get yoreself clothed an' I'll tell you,' said the old woman. 'I can't speak to a naked person.'

Jubal got dressed and settled down to listen. It was a curious revelation, because Mary Wilson settled into the chair beside the door and kept her back resolutely turned on him until he assured her he was fully clothed. It didn't seem to make any difference that she had seen him naked when she massaged his body: only that he should be clad as she spoke to him.

'I delivered Jane,' she said. 'When her momma got pregnant by Jason Wain. She was just a saloon girl back then, an' Jason was just a young cowboy come driftin' through. Only reason I ever knew Jane was his was the way she looked an' the way young Jase come back to find her.

'He had a whole wallet full o' money then, an' more in banks around the territory. Said he'd made it runnin' cows, but I doubt that. Anyway, he come back to Gillard an' announced he was settlin' down. He had enough money to buy himself a spread with some good breedin' cattle. He got his ranch started. Called it the Fat W, an' turned it into the biggest spread in the territory.

'Joanna was dead by then, an' the girl was three years old. Wild little creature, though I did what I could to raise her. Me an' Preacher Barns, an' old Jenny Tucker. They're both dead now. Died when Jane weren't more'n a slip. Her momma was long gone, drifted off to points north soon as she was able to travel, an' died someplace up north. There was a letter come back, tellin' how she didn't have nuthin' to leave except her love.

'That was around the time Jase come back, but I wouldn't let him have the kid, on account of him still being just a wild cowboy, no more'n a drifter, even though he did have money.

'Well, he settled in to building his spread. In fact, made it the biggest in these parts. But by then Jane was growed up into a pretty young woman. That was when Gil come around. He was one of Jason's cowboys, but he had an eye for the land an' he picked out that little valley fer his own. Some aunt back East left him some money, so he bought rights in the area. Staked the spread an' set to buildin' it up. Jason didn't like that, but Gil went right on. Told the old man he didn't have no claim on the land an' he was gonna make it even better than the Fat W.

'He even married young Jane. Which really upset Jason. He took her out to the cabin he'd built an' made the thing bigger. Jane was crazy wild in love with him. They summered, wintered an' springed out there. Built the place up to a real nice spread until Gil got ambitious.

'He set to building dams on the river. He said they was just to keep water back fer his own cows, but everyone knew they was holdin' the water off of Jason's land. He'd spread his holdings out a long ways by then, even set up a lumber mill in the hills. Gil's dams stopped the flow, so Jason started losin' money.

'He tried to buy Gil out, but Gil wouldn't listen. Seemed like he resented Jason from the start. Leastways, as soon as he heard how Jane was Jason's daughter. At the same time it seemed like Gil an' Jane was fixed on hurtin' the old man. An' that got worse when Laz Stoppard moved in.'

'Who's he?' Jubal stretched lazily on the bed, testing his muscles and finding them eased by the massage.

'Got a spread west of here,' said Mary Wilson. 'Borders on Jason's land, except they never did decide where the boundaries run. Fact is, Gil Last picked the best hunk of land he could find. Or the worst. That river flows down in two directions, so these dams he built can shunt water off from one spread to the other. That's why neither Jason nor Laz likes Gil bein' up there.

'Or liked,' she corrected. 'Him bein' dead, an' all. Fact is, that watercourse stays disputed, an' either way anyone helps Jane or Gil, they're upsettin' one o' the big ranchers.'

'All I want is to get to Blazeville,' said Jubal. 'After I find my money.'

'Best ask Billy Judge,' said the old woman. 'He's got his ear on the ground, so he picks up most of the shit.'

He went back to the stable. Billy Judge looked surprised to see him.

'I didn't think you'd come back,' he said. 'I thought you'd be long gone.'

'No.' Jubal shook his head. 'I got stopped on the way. Because someone talked about me.'

'Not me!' Billy Judge backed off with his head wagging and tobacco froth streaming down his jaws. 'I never told him you was going out.'

'Told who?' Jubal asked.

'No one,' said the old man, backing away down the stable. 'I swear it. No one.'

'Told who?' Jubal repeated, following the old man's retreat. 'Who'd you tell?'

The pain of his bruised body and the anger he felt at the beating clouded his words so that they came out from between tensed lips, emanating from a face that was masked with rage. His ugly visage frightened Billy Judge so that the oldster stumbled farther back down the aisle of the stable and began to moan as he watched the small man in the grey suit approach closer; like a panther stalking its prey.

'No one,' he mumbled. 'No one at all.'

'Who?' Jubal asked. 'Tell me.'

'No one.'

The old man barked a phlegmy stream of tobacco juice over the straw, his spectacles clouding as his eyes blinked tears. Jubal saw a hayfork leaning against a stall and picked up the implement. It was a yard long, with two tines curving round from the end of the pole.

He hefted the heavy fork and then stabbed it towards Billy Judge. The stablehand flattened against the stable's wall. Jubal powered forwards, driving the tines into the wood so that the old man's head was trapped.

Billy Judge swallowed hard and spilled urine in a dark stain over the front of his pants.

'Who?' Jubal asked again. 'Who'd you tell?'

'Oh, Jesus!' Billy Judge reached up to clutch the tines of the fork and then felt the dampness of his pants, and reversed the movement so that his hands clutched at the spreading wetness of his crotch. He was torn between fear and embarrassment.

Fear won, and he said, 'Joe Farmer an' Norm Clayton, that's all. No one else, I swear.'

'Thanks,' said Jubal. 'Thanks a lot.'

He left the old man pinned against the wall and went out from the stable into the side alley, heading for the marshal's office.

There was a deputy dozing inside. He woke up as Jubal came in, lifting his feet off the desk and trying to look efficient.

'Two men stole close on two thousand dollars from me,' Jubal said. 'I think they're called Joe Farmer and Norm Clayton. They beat me up and ran me out of town. I think they work for Jason Wain.'

'Jesus!' said the deputy. 'Two thousand? That much.'

'Yeah,' said Jubal. 'What you doing about it?'

The deputy stood up. He towered a good five inches over Jubal's small frame. And said, 'The marshal ain't here right now. So there ain't much I can do.'

'Where is he?' Jubal asked.

'You the feller brought Gil Last's wife in?' said the deputy. 'You that one?'

'Sure.' Jubal nodded. 'That was me. Where do I find the marshal?'

'Wouldn't bother if I was you, feller,' said the deputy. 'There ain't much joy you'll get. Right now he's taking a drink with Joe an' Norm.'

'Drink,' said Jubal, 'has a way of turning sour. When someone puts their foot in it.'

## CHAPTER FIVE

The Gillard Empire was crowded when Jubal walked back in. The kerosene lanterns hanging from the ceiling had been lit against the encroaching night and the fug of oily smoke rising from the blackened chimneys was combining with the pall of tobacco smoke lifting from the drinkers to wreathe the ceiling in a dense, blue-grey mist. The two barkeeps were busy, filling orders for the men bellied up against the long trestle and the girls who brought trays to the gaming tables. Jubal pushed through to the bar and ordered whisky. The young bartender stared at him in open-mouthed amazement.

'Jesus!' he said. 'Who trod on yore face?'

'You'll know when I find him,' grunted Jubal. 'The marshal in here?'

'Deke?' The barkeep looked worried. 'He's playin' cards.'

He pointed through the crowd, indicating a broad-shouldered man in a black suit. 'That's him there.'

Jubal nodded his thanks and took his drink over to the table. The lawman was shuffling the pack, blinking the smoke of his cheroot away as he concentrated on mixing the cards. Jubal guessed he was around six feet tall and well over two hundred pounds. The seams of his coat bulged across the shoulders and the black vest was opened to let a spill of belly swell against the shirt buttons. Rolls of excess flesh hung over the gunbelt on his waist. A Colt .45 was holstered across his belly, the gun dragged round so that the butt stuck up from under the fat. He had grey hair that was thinning on top, the strands plastered across the bald patch with brilliantine.

There were two other players.

One was a man around forty years old, his face seamed and weathered by exposure to the elements. He wore a blue cotton shirt and a leather vest, the bottom buttons fastened to hold the garment clear of the twin Colts holstered butt-forwards on his hips. He was devoid of hair, except for a thin moustache that added a little weight to his narrow lips. His eyes were hooded and cold blue mean, set close together either side of an axe-head nose.

The third man was younger. Maybe in his mid-twenties. He was dressed like a cowboy: denim work shirt and worn Levis. The cloth bulged with muscle. He carried a Remington Army model tied down on his right hip, the holster cut away far enough that the trigger was exposed. A sweat-stained stetson hung from the cord around his bull-like neck, revealing a wild tangle of dark brown hair that dangled about his collar. His eyes were a watery brown, and his mouth slacked open as he waited for the cards to be dealt, a moist, red tongue flicking over his lips.

There was an empty chair.

Jubal settled his left hand over the back and said quietly, 'You got a spare hand?'

None of the players had noticed him approach through the crowd. They looked up. And surprise spread over the faces of the two cowboys.

The lawman rolled his bulk around and grinned and said, 'Sure. New blood's always welcome.'

'That a fact?' Jubal asked, staring at the cowboys. 'That's good to hear.'

He sat down and the lawman dealt him in.

'Deke Tago,' he said. 'I represent the law in Gillard. What happened to yore face?'

'Seems like I upset someone,' Jubal murmured. 'Not every-one welcomes new blood like you, Marshal.'

'Talk about it later,' said Tago. 'Right now we're playin' poker. That's Joe Farmer.' He pointed at the bald man. 'An' Norm Clayton.'

'Pleased to meet you.' Jubal smiled, the expression settling his face into youthful lines that exposed the jagged edges of his broken teeth. 'What we playing?'

'Straight,' said Tago. 'Five cards with one change round. Fifty cents in the pot an' a limit of three dollars.'

'Suits me,' nodded Jubal. 'I lost enough today, already.'

Norm Clayton fidgeted in his chair. Joe Farmer picked up the bottle from the table and filled his glass, using the opportunity to nudge the younger man in the ribs. Jubal went on grinning and shook his head when the bottle came his way.

'My name's Cade,' he said quietly. 'Jubal Cade.'

Norm began coughing like the whisky had gone down the wrong way. Farmer just looked at Jubal without any expression on his face. Tago dealt cards.

Jubal collected two sevens, the Queen of Hearts, and two random cards. He bet on the first round and then changed the two wild ones. He got two equally useless, but put money in to see how the others handled things.

Tago won with two pairs: eights and tens.

Then Farmer took a hand with three of a kind, and the next with a full house. Clayton played loose – too nervous to concentrate – but still managed to pick up three hands with lucky cards. He took one on a flush; another with four of a kind; and the last with a six high straight.

Jubal had been playing carefully, allowing himself to lose along with Tago. He was around thirty dollars down, and the loss was beginning to nibble at his bankroll. From the money left out of his sojourn in Texas* the two cowboys had omitted to check his pockets – where he had kept five hundred dollars hidden.

He began to use them. Along with his expertise at cards.

He took the next hand on three sevens by pushing the bidding up. Then won the following round with a straight, nine high.

The round after that went to Farmer, but then Jubal took a

* *See JUBAL CADE no. 15 – ANGEL OF DEATH.*

full house and raised the betting to the limit. Farmer saw him: and lost fifty dollars.

It was more than any honest cowboy could afford to lose. More than any honest cowboy would own that side of the cattle drives or the spring round-ups.

Farmer's eyes got even more hooded, and under his peppery moustache his lips flattened to a thinner line. Clayton giggled. Tago lit a fresh cheroot.

Jubal went on winning. He parlayed three hearts into a flush and took seventy dollars from the pot. Then urged a set of three deuces up to a second full house. Overplayed a set of two pair to win a ninety dollar pot. Then took one hundred dollars with three of a kind and a King.

'Too much for me.' Deke Tago folded his hand. 'I ain't up to this style.'

Norm Clayton followed suit. 'Busted,' he said. 'I don't got no more money.'

Joe Farmer went on looking expressionless and said, 'Funny how some stranger walks into a game an' picks up the whole pot.'

Jubal totted his winnings: close on three hundred dollars. He counted them carefully, making sure that everyone seated around the table knew the exact amount.

'Not nearly close on eighteen hundred,' he said. 'Long way off that much.'

Norm Clayton replied before Farmer had a chance to stop him.

'You suggestin' sumthin', feller?'

Jubal shrugged. 'Heard you both work for the Fat W. I never knew cowboying paid so well.'

Norm jumped his chair back.

'Who told you that? Billy Judge?'

'You goddam fool! Why don't you keep yore goddam mouth shut?'

Joe Farmer didn't bother to stand up. He just crossed his arms over his waist and reached for his guns as he tilted his seat back to provide the space necessary for drawing the pistols.

Deke Tago shouted and reached for his own pistol, catching his hand in his vest and the flab overlaying the belt.

Jubal had his boot-heels settled firmly against the floor, ready for the movement. When it came, he straightened his legs so that his chair tipped over and powered sideways. He had already guessed that Joe Farmer would prove the faster draw, so he shot him first.

He fired while he was still falling, feeling the familiar triple *click!* of the hammer going back, then angling his shot up over the rim of the table to strike Farmer two inches above his belt, on the left side.

The bullet tore in through the man's lean belly. It ripped through his stomach and entered his heart. The left ventricle ruptured in a great spray of scarlet blood that splashed out over the upturned cards, then ricocheted from a rib to lodge beneath the scapula. Joe Farmer shouted. 'Oh, Christ! I'm dead.' And got lifted back off his feet.

He fell down with blood spilling from his mouth and both eyes wide open as they stared at the blankness of his death.

Jubal fired again.

Norm Clayton had the Remington out and pointed. But Farmer's falling body struck him and knocked his arm off balance. His shot ploughed chips from the card table, lifting Marshal Tago's glass up in a high arc that fluttered whisky down over the trajectory of the bullet.

Jubal's shot landed between the cowboy's eyes. It plunged his whole face into darkness as the bridge of his nose imploded through his brain. Both eyeballs popped clear of the sockets, leaving only pits that were full of blood and the sticky tendrils of the nerves. From the rear of his skull there gouted a wide column of blood that was flecked with sticky, grey brain matter.

A lantern shattered as the bullet hit the glass, dripping oil over the crowd. A girl screamed as she felt the mess of Norm Clayton's brain splatter over her breasts.

The cowboy staggered back, his body not yet ready to accept the fact of his dying. His pistol blasted a final shot that glanced off the ceiling and burst a bottle behind the bar. Like the bursting of his life.

Jubal fired again as the second bullet gouted from Norm's gun. He shot the cowboy in the stomach, landing his shot a few inches up from the belt and over to the left. Aiming it at the heart.

It doubled Norm over, bursting the heart and emerging from his back too spent to harm anyone, but still loosing sufficient blood to panic the onlookers and send them scurrying away.

The big cowboy crumpled over. His body hit the floor like a tree coming down, and he was still.

Jubal swung his gun to cover Marshal Tago.

The fat lawman shook his head and picked himself up from the floor. He was holding his Colt, but the hammer was down and his face was pale.

He shook his head again.

'No trouble, feller. Not so long as you can explain it. Besides, there's all these folk watching.'

Jubal nodded. 'Sure. I got no argument with you.'

He ejected the spent cartridges and reloaded his pistol. Dropped it back in the holster. Tago eased his bulk upright and said, 'We best talk this over. In my office.'

Jubal nodded again: 'Yeah. I want to know where my money went.'

'Follow me,' said Tago; straightening his hair and jacket as he tried to look in command of the situation. 'Down the block.'

Jubal followed him to the office. Tago sent the deputy off to cover some rounds and settled behind his desk.

'What was that about?' He held his Colt in his hand as he asked.

'They stole eighteen hundred dollars from me,' said Jubal. 'After they beat me up.'

'Proof?' demanded the lawman. 'I can't run you out o' town fer killin' 'em, but what proof you got?'

Jubal showed him the note and suggested he check the dead men's saddlebags. Tago shrugged at the note, and the bags were empty. Then Jubal suggested the bodies were checked.

Each one revealed a large amount of money. Added to what they had lost in the poker game the full amount came to almost eighteen hundred dollars.

'What proof I got this belongs to you?' asked Tago. 'Just yore word, so far.'

'You know any cowboys carry that kind of money?' Jubal demanded. 'There's nowhere else they'd get it, except trail robbery.'

'They work fer Jason Wain,' grumbled the fat peace officer. 'No tellin' what his boys get up to.'

'Your job to find out,' rasped Jubal. 'All I want is my money back and to get out of here.'

'You'll go if I give it you?' queried Tago. 'No questions asked?'

'Hell!' Jubal sighed. 'All I want to do is get out. I've been telling people that since I come here.'

'Where you goin'?' Tago sounded doubtful. 'Far away?'

'Blazeville,' said Jubal. 'I got word there's a man there I'm looking for.'

'Poor bastard,' murmured Tago. It was hard to tell if he meant the searcher or the victim. 'Tell you what. I'll give you the money if you agree to leave come morning.'

'I was trying to do that today,' said Jubal. 'You got a deal.'

The lawman breathed a sigh of relief and passed over the wadded notes. Jubal counted them: there were less than the original eighteen hundred, but his winnings from the poker game made up the difference.

'In the morning,' he said, tucking the bills inside his coat. 'After a night's sleep.'

'Fair enuff,' grinned Tago. 'Just so long as you ride straight through to Blazeville an' don't ever come back here.'

'Only reason I stopped in the first place was Last,' said Jubal. 'And he wasn't around long.'

'His wife will be,' grunted Tago. 'An' she ain't the end of our problems.'

'Yours,' said Jubal. 'Not mine. First thing I want to do is get a long way from anyone called Last.'

## CHAPTER SIX

It was early enough that the dining room was nearly empty, and Jubal ate quickly, eager to quit Gillard. There was no danger of legal repercussions, but he was anxious to avoid a run-in with any more of the Fat W hands. More anxious to put the town behind him and continue his delayed journey to Blazeville.

He drained the last of his coffee and settled his bill, then went over to the stable. Billy Judge was spitting tobacco outside, wrapped in a heavy plaid coat against the early cold. There was a narrow bruise across the front of his scrawny neck.

When he saw Jubal approaching he emptied a long stream of black liquid over the ground and climbed warily to his feet.

'You put yore pony back in when I weren't around.' His voice was hoarse, and he swallowed hard as he spoke, touching the bruise. 'An' you never paid.'

'Thought you owed me,' Jubal rasped. 'I paid you enough for the two nights.'

'That's different,' husked the old man. 'I ain't gonna make no money lettin' folks take their horses in an' out any time they fancy.'

'You shot your mouth off once before,' said Jubal, his voice hardening. 'You remember what happened?'

Billy Judge coughed and began to stroke his throat. Jubal spotted the pitchfork leaning against the wall and hefted the tool in his right hand before driving the tines hard into the frosted ground. The stablehand gulped and stood aside, his eyes riveted to the quivering shaft.

'Glad you take my point,' murmured Jubal. 'Now I'll get my horse.'

Inside the stable the big dog began to bark when it saw Jubal approaching. Its bushy tail swung furiously from side to side and its lolling tongue flicked from its lips. Jubal paused, stroking the massive head. The dog whined, licking his hand.

Jubal patted the animal. 'I guess you're lonely, Jim. It's a dog's life, but that's the way it goes.'

He saddled the pony and fastened his gear in place. Billy Judge turned his back as Jubal led the animal out of the stable and mounted. 'Were I you, feller, I wouldn't come back.'

'Don't aim to,' rasped Jubal. 'I keep telling people that.'

He reined in outside the general store and bought supplies. According to the directions he had received, Blazeville was around two days' ride away, so he kept his order to the minimum to avoid burdening the bay horse. While he was slinging the sacks over his saddle, Mary Wilson came up to him.

She had a thick broadcloth coat buttoned over her sparse frame, and a black shawl draped over her grey hair.

'You're going,' she said. 'Wisest thing.'

'You heard about last night?' Jubal paused with one foot in the stirrup. 'About the shooting?'

'Everyone has.' The old woman shrugged. 'Reckon by now Jason Wain's gettin' some of his boys together fer a party. The kind that ends with someone high. With nuthin' but a rope to hold him up.'

'Thought crossed my mind,' said Jubal. 'That's one reason I'm going.'

'Jane'd like to say goodbye. She appreciates what you done.'

Jubal grinned and shook his head. 'Tell her I appreciate her thanks, but I favour my neck even more. I hope she's all right.'

'I'll tell her.' Mary Wilson watched as he tugged the rein loose from the hitching rail, then placed a hand on his knee. 'I'll tell you sumthin' else: don't go out the same way.'

'It's the straightest route to Blazeville,' said Jubal, curious. 'Why not?'

'Takes you over Wain land,' said the old woman. 'Enuff folk know you come in that way fer Jason to have set guards out. Next time you mightn't be so lucky.'

'You got another route?' Jubal asked.

She nodded. 'Follow the west ridge round. It'll take you a few hours longer to pick up the trail, but you can make that up on the flat. That'll take you through Crazy Z country, but after what you done to Joe an' Norm, Laz Stoppard's boys ain't so likely to take offence. You just follow the west flank of the ridge until you hit three streams like fingers, then turn east an' north to the pass an' you'll be back where you started.'

'Seems like that's been happening a lot lately,' murmured Jubal, 'but thanks.'

He heeled the bay to a walk as the old woman called, 'See you round.'

'I hope not,' he muttered. And lifted the bay to a trot.

North of Gillard there were several trails bleeding out to the open country that led up to the ridges. The straight line Jubal had taken coming in pointed slightly east of north, so he swung round – taking Mary Wilson's advice – to the west of the pole point. It was a narrower path. Less used.

He climbed easily up the slope flanking Gillard and followed a wide swing that curved out due west before looping round to the north again. For the first few hours it was all grassland, the rising sun boiling the frost off the greenness so that a thin overlay of mist covered the plain. As the trail got steeper where it hit the foothills of the ridge the grass gave way to timber and the mist got thicker, hanging between the boles and the branches of the tall pines like fog painted on the backdrop of some theatrical production. Jubal shivered, pausing long enough to tug on the waterproof coat lashed to his saddle.

The trail wound up through the down flank of the ridge. Clear of the grass it got narrower still, and the ground got harder as stone took the place of soil. The bay pony slowed under Jubal's urging and its own inclination: visibility was down to around ten feet. The shod hooves rang loud, the clopping echoing through the trees like hammer blows.

Jubal hauled the Spencer out of the saddlebucket and carried the rifle canted over his saddle. He was still unsure of exactly whose land he was crossing. And equally unsure of exactly who might try to stop him. Or why.

The trail continued to angle upwards. In places it got narrower still as roots burst out from the high banks, forming tangled obstacles that jutted like the tentacles of an octopus across his path. They slowed him even more so that his pace came down to a reluctant walk. Natural caution prompted him to shift his head from side to side, listening for any unusual sounds.

He heard a bluejay scream and a crow croak. A squirrel chattered irritably, and two magpies set up a vicious squawling. Softer, there was the song of buntings and thrushes.

He tried to see through the mist, alternating his concentration between picking out the trail and scanning the dense-hidden area to either side.

Instinct, rather than the *click*! of the hammer cocking behind his back, prompted him from the saddle.

He went off to the left, foot slamming against the pony's shoulder so that the beast squealed and turned round. Blocking the trail. He landed on his side, the Spencer primed and angling through the fog as he rolled to the underhang of a large spread of roots.

'I'll not shoot. Less'n you make me.'

The voice was casual. Almost amused.

'Of course, if you do I can drop yore horse. After that you won't have no place to run.'

Jubal bellied down behind the roots. It was difficult to decide where the voice was coming from. The fog and the trees distorted sound almost as much as vision. He shouted an answer:

'What you want?'

A chuckle. Then: 'You the feller brought Jane Last in?'

'Yeah.' Jubal was getting tired of answering that question. 'I did.'

'An' then you killed Joe Farmer an' Norm Clayton?'

'Yeah,' Jubal shouted; wondering what was going on. 'In fair fight.'

'So I heard. You must be good – Joe Farmer was fast.'

'Not fast enough.' Jubal tried to pinpoint the voice as he slid backwards from the roots, seeking the better cover of a boulder. 'He's dead.'

'Won't be anyone mourns either o' them punks.' The voice was farther north now, the words lilting through the trees. 'They never was much. Just no-good gunhands.'

'And you?' Jubal looked at the bay pony, wondering if he could reach it and ride out fast enough to miss a bullet. 'What are you?'

'Good.' The voice had changed direction. Jubal twisted his head, trying to locate it. 'A very good gunhand. One of the best.'

It was hard to define the position anymore. The speaker had kept moving around, using the trees and the fog to mask his location. Speaking softly, then raising his voice, so that it was impossible to judge the exact distance or site.

'So how come I'm still alive?' Jubal hollered. 'Or aren't you quite that good?'

'Enough.'

The words came from behind him and he powered over, angling the Spencer up at the bank.

Then froze as he saw the muzzle of a Winchester jutting out from the roots wound round the boulder.

'Drop it!' The voice lost its laziness and got hard. 'You can't see me. You can't kill me. So drop it.'

Jubal set the Spencer down on the damp ground. He left the hammer cocked.

The voice chuckled. 'Stand up. You won't get a chance to reach the rifle. An' if you try for that Colt, I'll be forced to kill you.'

'Why not do it now?' Jubal asked. 'Try it.'

'Don't want to kill you. No one paid me fer that yet.'

The voice got louder as the man stood up.

He was around six feet tall, with long, straight brown hair hanging from under a flat-brimmed black stetson. He eased over the rim of the trail and slid down on his butt to face Jubal. He was young. Maybe in his twenties. But his eyes were cold under the amusement, and the Winchester was rock-stable on Jubal's chest. He was wearing an ankle-length coat of dull grey cloth, the shoulders and chest glistening moist with the fog. The coat was open so that Jubal could see the fancy vest he wore beneath. It looked to be picked out with silver threads, glistened over with damp so that it appeared metallic.

'Never did believe in killin' folks,' he grinned. 'Not unless they upset me. Or I got hired to do it.'

'So why stop me?' Jubal eased his elbows back against his coat, spreading the material clear of his waist. 'What for?'

'Curiosity, mostly,' said the gunman. 'I heard about you an' I wanted to take a look fer myself.'

'You heard and you looked,' Jubal rasped. 'Now what?'

'Guess you can ride on,' said the youngster. 'After I tell you a coupla things.'

For no particular reason other than instinct Jubal knew that the man was not planning to kill him. At least not now. Had he been a hired gun he would have completed his commission in the least possible time. Simply shot Jubal in the back and gone to claim his reward. Had he been another cowboy with a ready gun hand – like Joe Farmer or Norm Clayton – he would have used his gun again. Maybe giving Jubal a chance in order to justify the killing, but still pushing it farther than any man would allow. To provoke the fight.

This man didn't. He just stood there with his Winchester pointed at Jubal's chest and a smile on his face.

'What things?' Jubal asked.

'Jason Wain's gonna be lookin' fer you. Lookin' hard an' mean,' said the man. 'He ain't gonna rest until the feller who brought his daughter in gets killed. That shootin' in the saloon, that's not gonna help his feelings.

'Fact that you saved Gil Last's kid don't render you kindly to me. Be better if the thing had died. That'd make the whole affair a lot easier to sort out.'

He shrugged and ducked his head in the direction of Jubal's horse without moving the rock-steady Winchester.

'What I'm sayin' is you'd best ride on an' not come back. Not ever.'

'Jesus!' Jubal sighed. 'Doesn't anyone listen to me? That's all I want to do.'

# CHAPTER SEVEN

The Winchester lowered and the man's hand thumbed in the direction of his horse. Jubal climbed astride the bay. The gunman tossed him his rifle. After emptying the seven shot chamber.

Jubal bucketed the rifle and touched the brim of his derby.

'I hope we don't meet again.'

'Goes twice,' said the gunman. 'I kinda like you, but next time I might hafta kill you.'

'Yeah,' Jubal heeled the bay out into the mist. 'Same goes for me.'

He lifted the pony to a trot, riding on about one thousand yards. Then he stopped and reloaded the Spencer. From somewhere down the slope behind him he heard the beat of hooves against damp ground. They receded through the fog like memories getting lost under the weight of time. He rode on.

As the sun came up from under the hills the fog lifted. At first it was just a skirling of the mist, but then lances of sunlight danced through the trees and the sky above the pines got bright. Soon there was nothing but rays of light and dappled shadows, dust motes dancing in the air and birds singing. The trail wound down off the ridge, entering a wide meadow that was bordered on its western flank by a series of low hills, to the north by a narrow pass. A stream cut clear of the eastern ridge to spill down the flank and bleed its water over the meadow.

Jubal noticed that the outpouring seemed thinned. The banks of the stream were wider than the flow, the water making a narrow track down between walls of bare rock and outcrops of lichen. Where it struck the meadow the banks were drying out, yellow mud contrasting with the green of the grass, the angles getting silted up as the dying trickle failed to wash them clean.

Up ahead he saw a shimmer of water that he guessed came from the fingers Mary Wilson had described. He rode towards them.

By now the day was warm. Out from the timber the fog was dispelled by the breeze, and the sun was shining the full breadth of the valley. Frogs croaked in the stream, and wagtails ducked their plumage over the mud revealed by the drying banks. The valley smelled lush and rich with that sweet scent that comes from moistened grass when the sun hits it. Jubal took off his coat and stowed it back on his saddle. He glanced at his watch: fifteen minutes off eleven; and spurred the bay pony forwards.

Cattle grazed in the meadow, raising lazy heads as he passed by. They looked fat, ready to face the coming winter. He grinned as he rode through them, angling the horse towards the distant pass.

As he got closer he saw that it was little more than a cut in a bowl of rock. The sides lifted up a thousand feet or more, scrub growing from the higher reaches and pines topping the rimrock. The grass ceased a few hundred feet up from the bed of the valley and after that the flanks got bare. The high edges filled the bottom with shadow so that the vee-shape of the cut took on the appearance of a knife's edge, its rim stained with blood.

He splashed through the three streams, noticing that each one was low, revealing pale banks all dappled with dried-out pebbles and sun-dried water weeds.

He halted beside the northernmost fork and let the bay drink as he chewed on hardtack. The sun was warm now. Comforting, after the dampness of the tree-lined fog, and he let it soak into his clothes and his bones, enjoying it.

When he was finished eating he mounted again and rode on towards the forbidding pass. It was some time after noonday, but the high angles of the ridges cast permanent shadow over the bottomlands. As though guarding the exit from the valley. Cattle shifted from his coming, but he noticed that none went near the exit passage.

As he rode closer, he saw why.

There was a gate built across the pass. It was best part of ten feet high, rough-cut pine limbs angled over uprights that were sunk into the ground. Beyond the gate an area of fifty feet or so had been burned out and forked over with some kind of salt chemical. Lye, or something similar. The soil was dead: parched and leprous white. Nothing grew there, and none of the cows cropping the lush grass around ventured near.

There was a narrow gate at the centre. One just wide enough to allow a wagon entrance. It was fastened to the enormous uprights on either side of the trail by massive chains.

Two men guarded it.

They lifted their carbines in Jubal's direction as he approached. He raised both hands above his head and called, 'I'm going north. To Blazeville. Let me through?'

A Winchester angled on his face as the mouth behind called, 'You're on Stoppard land. Why?'

Jubal sighed, urging the bay pony on with his feet; keeping his hands up over his head.

'I didn't want to ride through the Fat W country,' he said. 'All I want is to get to Blazeville, and someone told me I could get there faster this route.'

'Who?' The voice was dry, hidden behind the carbine. 'Who told you that?'

'An old lady,' said Jubal. 'Mary Wilson. She said you'd let me through.'

The face behind the gun crackled with laughter: 'You're the feller brought Jane Last in to Gillard, ain't you?'

'Oh shit,' grumbled Jubal, 'here it goes again.'

'What?' The man stood up. He was around Jubal's age, but worse lined. 'What you say?'

'Nothing,' said Jubal. 'Yeah, I took her in. She was pregnant. Needed somewhere to have her baby in comfort with her husband dead.'

'Gil's dead?' The man whooped. 'Now ain't that good news? You better come with us, feller.'

'I'm going to Blazeville,' said Jubal. 'I been trying to leave Gillard these last few days. I don't want to go anywhere else. Except Blazeville.'

'I got somethin' here says you do like I say,' called the guard. 'There's another like it to the side. An' two more on the rocks. You want to go on arguin', you just see how we reply.'

Jubal looked up. Two men had emerged from the boulders either side of the pass now; both held Winchesters pointed on him. There was a fourth man come out from the gate. He held a Winchester, too.

'You called it,' Jubal allowed. 'Let's go.'

The first speaker shouted orders to his companions and the gate was opened wide enough to let a piebald gelding through. The man swung into the saddle and the gate slammed shut again. The chains rattled as they were fastened back in place. The Winchester stayed pointed on Jubal's face.

'Stay in front,' warned the cowboy. 'Don't try nuthin'. I ain't in no mood to dig a grave.'

'I'm in a big enough hole already,' muttered Jubal, then louder: 'Where we going?'

'To have a talk with Laz Stoppard,' grunted the cowboy. 'Figger he's got some questions to ask you.'

Jubal shrugged and heeled his pony forwards. The cowboy stayed ten feet behind him, calling directions, his carbine held steady on Jubal's spine. They followed the line of the northern ridge, skirting the perimeter of the meadow until a narrow trail showed in the rock. Then they cut upwards, riding clear of the grass until they were following a slender path that angled steadily towards the rimrock. Before they reached the top the cowboy shouted for Jubal to turn off the path and follow the game trail that wound through the pines. This route was even narrower than the earlier path. Branches hung low across their passage, and roots threatened to foul the cautious stepping of the two horses. Jubal thought about trying to make a break, but decided that he was too easy a target. Besides, he was beginning to feel curious about the interest shown in him.

The idea of two cattlemen contesting land was nothing new. Nor the resentment of a homesteader closing off water that could make the difference between life and death for the cattle; between profit and loss for the ranchers. What was odd was the interest in Jane Last's impending birth and the hostility towards Jubal for saving the woman and her unborn child. He wondered if Laz Stoppard would shed any light on the situation.

Meanwhile, he concentrated on the trail. The game path was winding now, running along the flank of a counter-angled valley towards a fresh spread of grass-filled meadowland. There were even more cows here than in the first bowl, the heavy bovine heads lifting as the two riders approached, the fleshy lips parting to chorus their passage through the herd with a dull, lowing rumble of sound.

They passed over the meadow and climbed another ridge. It was lower than the others, cut through at the centre with the bed of a long-dried river. Where once the water had run, there was now a covering of wind-blown dirt that sprouted small plants and patches of moss. Halfway along it curved off to the north and the cowboy ordered Jubal to climb the bank, in a westerly direction.

By now it was late afternoon and the sun was getting lower in the sky. The valleys behind them were already filling up with darkness, and in the east the horizon was getting tinged with greenish black.

Jubal crested the ridge and stared at the panorama spread below him. The sun was shining directly into his face, its radiance filling the enormous bowl of land spread out before him like a green sea lit with burning gold. Halfway down the mile-long slope the trees had been cut away, the dead timber used to construct a series of terraces that would catch the rootless dirt when it dried out and crumbled into landspills. Shoots of green plucked upwards through the soil where crops of vegetables had been planted, and the stream bleeding out from the north was channelled so as to feed each terrace. Lower down there was just grass, almost hidden beneath the enormous weight of cattle cropping there. Far off, coursing down the centre of the valley, was a stream that shone silver-blue in the waning light. Beyond it, the indistinct bulk of a ranch.

'Move it.' The cowboy's grunt reminded Jubal of the carbine at his back. 'You ain't sight-seein'.'

They rode down the slope, their descent taking them through layers of light that grew progressively darker as they approached the bottomlands and the sun faded deeper behind the western hills.

By the time they hit the river the lower slopes were in darkness and lights were shining from the buildings ahead. The cowboy pointed Jubal to a well-worn road that lifted over a series of grassy undulations towards a tall fence. There was a gate set into the timber with a lean-to at the side. A rickety-looking structure of poles and ladders lifted up about fifteen feet from the ground directly beside the lean-to. It reminded Jubal of the watchposts he had seen in Army stockades.

The cowboy ordered him to halt and hollered up at the tarpaulin-covered structure.

'Cole Brandon comin' through with a feller Laz wants to see.'

'Go ahead, Cole.'

The answering voice echoed eerily out of the darkness.

Brandon shouted, 'Keep him covered.' And rode ahead to swing the gate open. He backed his piebald against the frame as Jubal went through, then eased the gelding forwards and clear of the gate, letting it swing closed on its own momentum before riding back into step behind Jubal.

The path went straight up to the crest of a low rise in the otherwise flat ground. A quarter mile on there was a lower fence, not guarded, and beyond, the lights of the ranch house shone through the twilight.

As they came closer, Jubal saw the ranch was built in a circular configuration around the peak of the hill. Mostly it was just one level from the ground, but in three places the linkage of buildings was joined by towers that lifted around thirty feet into the air. Like the rest of the houses, the towers were built of stone, roofed over with timber, but – unlike the main buildings – dark. He saw the dim red glow of a match flame reflected off the overhanging wood of the nearest tower, its light glancing off a rifle barrel.

'It's Cole!' shouted the cowboy. 'Where's the boss?'

'Inside,' came the answer. 'Who you got with you?'

'Feller took Jane Last in to Gillard,' called Brandon. 'Thought the boss'd want to talk with him.'

'Christ!' The guard sounded surprised. 'Thought he'd be long gone.'

'Woulda been if he didn't ride straight into the north fence,' called Brandon. 'Like a goddam fly into a spider web.'

The guard chuckled and Brandon said for Jubal to dismount.

They were in front of the single largest building in the circle, a tall, wide house with long windows set into the stone, fancy ironwork covering the glass and a big door at the exact centre. Several cowboys came wandering through the shadows under the porch, and Brandon tossed the reins of his horse to the nearest man.

Another cowboy took Jubal's horse, grunting in surprise as the small man in the grey derby snatched his medical valise from the saddle.

'What the hell you got in there?' Brandon demanded. 'Show me.'

'Medical stuff,' said Jubal. 'Nothing more.'

'Show me.' Brandon's voice got ugly. 'Right now.'

The Winchester came up to point on Jubal's face again, so he opened the bag. Brandon peered inside, his weatherbeaten face creasing into even more lines as he saw the array of phials and scalpels and liniments.

'Looks like he's a doctor, Cole.'

The voice was deep with authority, and the light that spilled out from the opening door added a dramatic note to the statement. Brandon looked up and doffed his stetson.

'Found him on the north fence, boss. He's the one took Jane Last into Gillard.'

'That a fact?' said Laz Stoppard. 'What about Gil?'

'Says he's dead,' Brandon replied. 'Says he found him dying an' then took Jane in to town. I reckoned you'd want to talk with him.'

'Yeah. Bring him inside. Leave him his bag, but check his gun.'

Stoppard turned around and went back into the house before Jubal got a chance to see him clearly. Brandon shoved the carbine up against his stomach and fetched the Colt from the holster. A second cowboy ran hands over Jubal's suit and pronounced him clean of other weapons.

'Step on in,' said Brandon.

Jubal climbed onto the porch, blinking as the light from inside the room hit his eyes. It was a big room, with a polished pine floor and tapestries hung over the stone walls. A fireplace occupied half of the inner wall, and doors shone gleaming with polish on either side. There was a vast table at the centre, surrounded by about fifteen carved oak chairs, with a silver candelabra in the middle and a matching silver tray with fancy goblets alongside.

Laz Stoppard was stooped over a glass-fronted cupboard, pouring drink from cut crystal decanters into cut crystal glasses. He was around fifty years of age, with the kind of leanly muscular body that comes from working long hours in the saddle. His hair was thick, but grey, curling over the collar of a yellow shirt. He wore tight-fitting corduroy pants that dragged over the heels of darker brown boots. The shine on the boots contrasted with the dullness of the corduroy. When he turned round, Jubal saw that his face was near as brown as his boots, with blue eyes sparkling from the tan and tobacco-stained teeth matching the colour of his shirt. A long scar spoilt his handsomeness: it ran down from the left temple to the eye, tugging the orb into a squint before continuing along the cheek to the side of his mouth. That side was puckered in a fixed grin.

The scar shone pale white against the tan. Stoppard smiled. It was an eery smile, because only the right side of his face showed it. The left side went on grinning its fixed smile, confusing natural humour with the rigidity of the scar-fixed grimace.

'Whisky?' he asked.

'Thanks.' Jubal set his bag on the table and took the glass. 'Thanks a lot.'

'You must be pretty angry,' said Stoppard. 'It's understandable, but I hope I can make it up to you.'

'That's easy,' Jubal replied. 'Let me go.'

'Where?' Stoppard lifted his glass in a toast. 'Cole Brandon's not the most delicate man I employ, but he was only doing what he thought was his duty. Eat with us.'

'The only reason I'm here,' said Jubal, 'is because I was heading for Blazeville. I don't know a damn' thing about your trouble with Jason Wain, or anything about his daughter. I just found her husband dying and took him home.'

'No more than any other decent man would have done,' said Stoppard. 'I'd have done the same myself in your situation. Are you really a doctor?'

The abrupt change took Jubal by surprise.

He nodded. 'Sure. You want to see the certificate.'

Stoppard shook his scarred head. 'No. I saw the bag. No reason anyone would carry that unless he knew something about the profession. Why didn't you deliver the baby in the cabin?'

'She wasn't ready,' said Jubal. 'And I didn't want to wait around. It seemed like it was a better idea to get her into Gillard and let Mary Wilson handle the birth.'

'So the child is there?' asked Stoppard; innocently. 'With the midwife?'

'Depends,' answered Jubal, 'on if it's born yet. When I left, it wasn't.'

'And you made no depositions?' asked Stoppard. 'Signed no papers?'

Jubal shook his head. 'No. I just took the woman to the midwife and left her there. I did all I could. She's not my problem – all I want is to get to Blazeville.'

'And no one stopped you?' said Stoppard. 'You had no trouble with the Fat W?'

'I got beaten up,' Jubal allowed; curious. 'Two cowhands roughed me and stole my money.'

'What happened?' asked the scar-faced man. 'After that?'

'I went back,' said Jubal. 'I got my money back.'

'And the two cowhands?' Stoppard said. 'What about them?'

'Dead,' Jubal answered. 'I killed them.'

Stoppard nodded and sipped his whisky. 'How much did they take from you?'

'About eighteen hundred,' said Jubal.

'But you got it back?'

'I told you I did.' Jubal felt that he was in some kind of test. 'That's why I took the long road to Blazeville. Over your land.'

'Who did you kill?' asked Stoppard, refilling their glasses. 'What were their names?'

'Joe Farmer and Norm Clayton,' Jubal answered. 'Why?'

'What did they look like?' asked Stoppard, avoiding the immediate question. 'Tell me?'

Jubal described them, intrigued by the way the rancher shook his head and frowned a half-faced grimace.

'No one else?' he asked. 'No one with long brown hair and a fancy vest?'

Jubal remembered the gunman who had stopped him on the trail out of Gillard, and nodded.

'He killed three of my men,' said Stoppard. 'I heard he killed four of Jason's, too. Why not you?'

'He said it wasn't personal,' said Jubal. 'Had no reason to kill me.'

'I don't understand it,' said the rancher. 'Not that.'

'Nor me,' Jubal shrugged, 'so how about letting me go?'

'Later.' Stoppard waved his hand in the air and began to pour fresh drinks. 'You'll stay for the night, at least.'

'Suppose I don't want to?' Jubal asked. 'Can I go?'

Stoppard smiled and shook his head.

Jubal sat down and drank his whisky.

'They named Gillard wrong,' he murmured. 'They should have called it Blind Alley.'

## CHAPTER EIGHT

'Come with me.' Stoppard opened a door, motioning for Jubal to follow him. 'There's something I want to show you.'

Jubal stood up, trailing the rancher into a side room that was obviously used as an office. There was a roll-top bureau at the centre with a swivel chair behind it; cowhide rugs covered the floor, and most of one wall was taken up with a close detail map of the area.

'Smoke?' Stoppard lifted a humidor. Jubal took a cigar.

The room was dark and warm, filled with the odour of leather and smoke. Stoppard lit the kerosene lantern hanging from the ceiling and adjusted the flame until the whole room was bright. He went over to the map and touched a finger to a point left of the centre.

'That's where we are now,' he said. 'The Crazy Z main ranch. These are my boundaries.'

He traced a crude rectangle with his finger. Jubal noticed that the nails were bitten and grimed with dirt. The rectangle was bordered by the Niobrara river in the north and the Platte in the south. To the west the Wyoming line marked the edge; to the east, a range of nameless hills. It was a vast area.

'Wain's got about one third more,' said Stoppard. 'Good land. Just as good as mine.' He indicated an area eastwards and south of his own holdings. 'There's just one snag.'

He beckoned Jubal closer, pointing to a spot directly between the two ranches. The boundaries of the Crazy Z were marked in green, those of the Fat W in red. East of the dot that represented the ranch, the boundary line bulged inwards. So did the red lines. The inward curving formed an oval shape, across which several blue lines were drawn.

'That's – that *was* – Gil Last's homestead.' Stoppard flicked ash into a tray. 'Jason started before me, of course, but when I came along we had an arrangement that neither one of us would claim that land. Then Gil bought it.'

His voice got bitter.

'We got along until then, but Gil fouled it all up. I guess you've heard about him an' Jane?' Jubal nodded. Stoppard continued: 'The marriage upset Jason enough, but when Gil began cutting off the water, he went crazy. See?'

He ran a stubby nail down the blue lines.

'These are rivers an' streams. We both got enough water to the north an' south, but that's mostly on open land. Way the winter hits up here, we need real good, protected country to fatten our cattle. We're already bringing them in to graze them up ready for the winter, and for that we need good water. Gil staked his claim damn' centre of the most reliable water source we had. That's why neither one of us took possession: we both knew it'd mean a range war. Gil settled dead centre of that tract an' set to building dams so that he'd control our supply.'

Stoppard paused, emptying his glass. He went back into the outer room and returned with the decanter.

'We tried to buy him out, but he wouldn't listen. We tried to frighten him out, but he held on. He had legal right, of course, but the planners back East who sold him the land never did work out what it could mean. And neither Jason or me could risk taking his spread over. He was sitting pretty, especially with Jason's daughter for his wife.'

'You got your problems,' said Jubal, 'but they're not mine.'

'You're involved, though,' Stoppard answered. 'Whether you like it or not.'

'How?' Jubal shrugged. 'Last is dead now. His widow's not likely to try handling the place on her own, so you can buy her out.'

Stoppard shook his head. 'It's not that easy. Soon as Gil knew that Jane was pregnant, he drew up a will. He figgered that Jason would leave his spread to his daughter. Even if he didn't, there'd be a sound case for Jane claiming the land on next of kin rights. So Gil put everything in the baby's name. He had folks somewhere back East, so the will cut Jason out of any control. It left us right back where we started.'

'So who killed Gil?' asked Jubal. 'Doing that just seems to have complicated things.'

'You're goddam right!' Stoppard nodded. 'It's left me an' Jason fighting. That's why the baby is so important: whoever gets custody can control that land.'

'So argue it in court,' grunted Jubal. 'I got problems of my own.'

'But you found Gil,' said Stoppard, fingering his scar. 'Didn't he say anything to you?'

Jubal shook his head. 'He wasn't doing much talking. Just a lot of bleeding.'

'So he was unconscious when you took him home?'

Stoppard filled their glasses.

'He was dying,' said Jubal. 'That was all he had time for. He never woke up.'

'So he might have said anything?'

It was a suggestion. It set Jubal thinking.

Stoppard smiled at the momentary pause and went over to the bureau. Producing a key from his pants pocket, he opened the scroll top and lifted out a brass moneybox. A second key opened the box and he began to peel notes onto the polished surface of the desk. Jubal counted one thousand, in hundreds.

'Like what?' he asked.

'Like he changed his mind about the will,' said Stoppard, smiling his lop-sided grin. 'That he told you the child wasn't his and he didn't want it to get the homestead.'

He went on peeling notes as he spoke. Jubal watched him count off a second thousand before he shook his head.

'No deal,' he said. 'Whatever Last fixed up, you sort it out.'

'For God's sake, man!' The smile left Stoppard's face and got replaced by an ugly look. 'I'm offering you two thousand dollars to sign a piece of paper.'

'That's the trouble.' Jubal ground out his cigar. 'That piece of paper could tie me up in Gillard for months. You'd need a circuit judge to ratify it, and after that you'd have legal arguments.'

'Three thousand.' Stoppard dragged more bills from the box. 'That should cover it.'

'Mister,' grunted Jubal, 'I don't have the time. All I want is to get to Blazeville. The faster I put Gillard behind me, the better.'

'Four thousand,' snarled Stoppard, his face ugly as the mobile side twisted down to match the scar. 'My last offer.'

Jubal shook his head.

'No. I hate turning down that much money, but I just want to get out of here.'

'You may change your mind.' The rancher filled his own glass. 'I may just make you.'

He capped the decanter, and when his hand came up from the desk it held a Derringer. The hammer was cocked and the ugly black bore of the muzzle was fastened on Jubal's chest. His face was contorted with anger, lips drawn back from the stained teeth and eyes blazing. It matched the rage on Jubal's face as he reached instinctively for his gun and found his holster empty.

Stoppard laughed and shouted, 'Cole! Eli! Get in here.'

The outer door opened and boots thudded over the floor. The cowboy who had brought Jubal to the ranch came into the office with a hulking giant behind him. The second man was one of the biggest Jubal had ever seen. He ducked his head as he came in, shifting his body sideways in a way that suggested he was used to finding doors too narrow to accept the width of his shoulders. Strands of greasy blond hair tangled over his collar, spilling out from under a sweat-stained kepi that had once held the insignia of the Confederate Army. His denim work shirt was rolled up over folds of fat, the sleeves open at the cuffs to expose the matted hair covering his enormous wrists. The fingers looked too big to handle the shotgun that was holstered like a Colt on his waist.

Brandon had changed his Winchester for a Colt .45. It was

out and cocked, pointing at Jubal's face. He was smiling.

'He doesn't like my idea,' said Stoppard. 'Take him out and try to persuade him.'

'What if he keeps refusin', boss?'

Brandon asked the question. The giant just grinned and began to knead his fingers together. It was like watching bananas mashed.

'Kill him,' said Stoppard. 'Then dump him on Wain's land.'

'Right.' Brandon moved round in front of the desk, holding the Colt steady on Jubal's face. 'Eli?'

The giant moved forwards. Jubal noticed that his eyes were baby blue, and vacant as a dry stream. It was as though he had grown too fast, his body outstripping all other faculties. There was a loose blandness to his face, as though it was not yet fully formed. The nose was a wide spread that ended over sausage-like lips surrounded by a thin layer of wispy hair. His movements were ponderous, like a sheet of ice tugging loose from a stream's bank.

Jubal decided to take a chance. He watched the giant move towards him and backed away. As he shifted, he circled to his left, putting Eli's body between him and the two guns. Then he powered forwards, driving his skull hard against the ponderous belly.

It was like diving into a wall of rubber.

His chin grated on Eli's belt buckle, and the shock rippled waves of pain down through his neck and shoulders. Then he was grasped by the arms. Lifted upright so that he was staring straight into the huge cowboy's eyes. Eli chuckled and batted his face forwards. Sparks burst like rockets in Jubal's mind. He tasted blood on his tongue, then felt his feet hit the floor as the giant let him go. He slammed a fist against the man's crotch and stamped a heel over Eli's foot.

Eli chuckled some more and swung a hand, open-palmed, against Jubal's head.

Sound burst like thunder inside his skull. He felt his teeth snap closed over his tongue. Light flashed across his eyes. And he was down on the floor, listening to the giant's laughter.

From somewhere a long way off, he heard Stoppard say, 'Take him out now. Don't tell anyone else. And don't kill him unless I give the word.'

Then he was picked up like a baby and carried out of the room. He thought he heard a woman gasp, but decided it was his imagination. Felt chill air on his face, numbing the cuts on his lips and tongue. He was vaguely conscious of being carried over a courtyard; of a door opening. And then he was falling, fetching up with a sickening, dulling thud against something cold and hard.

And the beating began.

Darkness filled his mind and he curled into a tight ball, allowing unconsciousness to take away the pain.

He woke to dim light. It filtered in through a window high up in the wall, pale with the chill of early dawn. Dust motes danced in the light, and he saw that he was in some kind of store house. The walls were stone and the door – when he staggered to it – was of solid wood, locked on the outside. The window was located to the right of the door. A narrow slit cut too high up to reach, letting in just enough light that he could see his surroundings.

He was starting to explore when the door opened and Eli and Brandon came in.

'You want to do like the boss asks?' demanded the smaller man.

'Go to hell,' Jubal snarled.

Brandon slapped Eli on the back and the giant shambled forwards.

Jubal backed away. Brandon laughed, and Eli spread his arms like a bear. Like a grizzly. He came forwards faster than Jubal expected, weaving from side to side so that there was nowhere left to run. He caught Jubal and picked him up and squeezed him. Exactly like a grizzly: Jubal felt the air crushed from his lungs and thought his ribs would break. He was beginning to black out when the giant let him go. And kicked him as he fell.

After that there was nothing but pain. He was aware of being lifted up in one massive hand and struck with the other. He tasted blood in his mouth. Felt it run sticky down his face. Felt it trickle under his collar. Felt pain.

After a while it went away.

He became numb: unfeeling.

He woke again and it was dark. He was curled in a ball against the rearward wall, knees drawn up to his chest and his arms wrapped round to clutch his head. There was no feeling left in his jaw, but when he touched it, his hand came sticky with blood. His ribs and legs ached, and his left eye was swollen almost shut.

He groaned and went back to sleep, back into the welcome oblivion.

When he woke next he was hungry, the dull ache in his belly matching the pain of his bruised body. It was light again, and he examined his prison.

He was inside a room about fifteen feet by fifteen. The floor was hard stone, like the walls, the roof a thatched shadow too high above him to reach. Wooden piles supported it on both sides, but they were smooth and devoid of any handholds. There was a beam running across under the thatch, but it was a good fifteen feet from the floor, and his body ached too much to let him stand upright, let alone try to jump for that precarious exit route.

He curled back against the wall and watched the sun get brighter through the window.

After a while Brandon and the giant came back. Eli was carrying a plate of food that he set down on the floor. Brandon said, 'You changed yore mind yet?'

Jubal shook his head.

'You're a damn' fool,' grunted the cowboy. 'Eat some an' think about it.'

'I'll not change my mind.' Even to himself, Jubal's voice sounded thick; heavy with pain and blood.

'We ain't gonna wait too long,' said Brandon. 'That goddam

woman's about ready, so you put yore name on that paper or you die. You think about that.'

Jubal thought about it while he ate. He couldn't taste the food because his gums were bleeding and the bruising on his throat and stomach made it difficult to swallow. He ate because he knew he needed the sustenance. Knew that he needed the strength the food would give to support the hate in his mind.

When he was finished, he limped over to the door and pounded on the wood.

Brandon opened the door. It opened outwards, so that Jubal fell face down over the step. Brandon chuckled and nudged him with a boot.

'You changed yore mind?'

'Yeah.' Jubal stayed down on the ground, staring around the interior of the Crazy Z ranch. 'Take me to Stoppard.'

The ranch was built as he had thought on first impression. It occupied the knoll of a hill, the buildings spread in a circle around the crest. His prison was at the far end, opposite to the main house, one of a series of store sheds and bunkhouses and stables. The central area was paved, with a well at the centre and an interior porch running the full circle of the buildings. He tried hard to memorize the lay-out before Brandon called for Eli to pick him up and carry him to the office.

The giant dumped him unceremoniously on the stoop outside, grinning down as Brandon went in to alert Stoppard. Jubal crouched down, nursing his pain until the cowboy called for the giant to bring him in.

Eli lifted him to his feet and set his derby untidily on his head.

'I never wanted to mess you,' he mumbled. 'I just do what I'm told.'

It was the first time he had spoken.

'Yeah,' Jubal mumbled. 'You just do what a man's got to do.'

'I never heard that before,' said Eli, 'but I think you're right.'

## CHAPTER NINE

Stoppard was seated at the bureau, puffing on a cigar with an expression of barely controlled impatience clouding his face. He was staring at the middle-aged woman facing him across the desk. She had once been attractive, and even now would have looked handsome were her eyes not swollen and red with weeping and her mouth screwed into a nervous line. It was obvious that she had been arguing with Stoppard, and from the look on both their faces, she had lost.

The rancher made an impatient gesture and she rose to her feet, twisting a lace handkerchief into a tight ball between both hands. She glanced at Jubal and winced. For a moment it seemed that she was going to say something, but then she stopped herself, turning back towards Stoppard.

'You're wrong, Laz. It can't work.'

'Leave us, Mary.' His voice was cold, and it was only afterthought that added, 'Please.'

The woman shook her head in frustration and quit the office. The rancher motioned for Brandon to shut the door.

'My wife,' he murmured, 'does not agree with my plan.'

'The little feller does,' Brandon grinned. 'Now.'

'I thought you would.' Stoppard fixed Jubal with an incurious stare. 'Sit down.'

Jubal slumped into the chair, fighting the anger that gripped him. It was tempting to allow the fury to possess him. To permit the rage to power him forwards in an attempt to reach Stoppard. The rancher sensed his mood, for he waved Eli and Brandon in closer, reminding Jubal of the odds against him. Jubal recognized the senselessness of trying anything now and did his best to relax his aching body.

'You should have taken my offer first time round,' said

Stoppard. 'Now you wind up doing the same thing for nothing.'

'And after?' Jubal's voice was choking. 'What happens then?'

'You wanted to get to Blazeville,' said Stoppard. 'I'll send you there. After you done what I asked, Cole an' Eli here will take you across my land. I won't do a thing to stop you. I'll even keep the Fat W people off your back.'

'Thanks,' grated Jubal, cynically. 'Thanks a lot.'

Stoppard shrugged, smiling with half his face, and tapped a sheet of paper. 'This is a deposition I made up. It says that before Gil Last died he told you the child wasn't his, an' he didn't want it getting his homestead. He also said he didn't want Jane to have it, so the place should be sold off. That's pretty fair, ain't it? Jane an' the kid can make enough outta the sale to settle someplace else.'

'Still leaves you problems,' Jubal remarked. 'What about Wain?'

'That's the funny part,' grinned Stoppard. 'Poor ole Jason's put so much into the Fat W that he don't have enough spare cash to buy the Last place. I can outbid him, so I wind up owning the water all legal.'

'Clever,' Jubal allowed. 'Real clever.'

'Ain't I?' Stoppard's grin got as smug as his scar would allow. 'Now all you gotta do is ride back to Gillard an' tell all this to Deke Tago. Cole'll bring the banker in as a witness, an' Deke'll make the other. You sign this paper in front of 'em, an' then the boys'll take you to the north line. From there, it's not more'n a day to Blazeville.'

'You're pretty trusting,' grunted Jubal. 'Suppose I just tell Tago about all this?'

Stoppard laughed and shook his head. 'Deke's no hero. Why'd you think he gave you your money back an' let you go? He don't want trouble. Not with the Fat W, nor with me. Besides, I got a separate little document specially for him. A kinda thank-you note.'

He folded a second sheet of paper into an envelope. Followed it with a wad of bills.

'How about the banker?' Jubal asked. 'You got him sewn up, too?'

'Henry Carter?' Stoppard laughed some more. 'I'm his biggest depositor. Besides, he'll handle the sale an' take a commission on it. He'll go along.'

Jubal would have shrugged if his shoulders weren't hurting so much. Instead, he just nodded. Which made his neck ache. 'You got it all worked out,' he said.

'You're damn' right,' grinned Stoppard. 'Now let's get it moving.'

'No,' said Jubal. 'Not yet.'

'What the hell d'you mean?' The grin froze on the rancher's face. 'You want some more treatment from Eli?'

'No.' Jubal shook his head slowly. 'I mean it's a long day's ride to Gillard and I'll not make it. I need some rest.'

He wondered if the plan he had formulated would work. If it could work, given his weakened condition. Even if Stoppard took the bait he was dangling before the rancher's nose.

'Look,' he added, slurring his words even more than the beatings necessitated, 'right now I'm in a mess. I'd have trouble staying on a horse riding round a pasture, and the way back to Gillard's over some rough country. If I show up there looking like this, you might just have trouble proving that deposition is honest.'

'Yeah.' Stoppard frowned. 'You got a point.'

'I need about ten hours in a soft bed,' said Jubal, pressing his advantage. 'And my medical bag. I can fix myself up enough that Tago and Carter won't notice. Nor anyone else.'

Stoppard thought about it for a few moments that seemed to last hours. Then: 'All right. What d'you want?'

'A quiet room and a bed,' said Jubal. 'A good, hot bath. Bandages. My bag. Food. Mostly quiet.'

'You got it.' Stoppard nodded reluctantly. 'I'll give you until the morning. Don't try anything fancy, though. There'll be a man outside your door all the time.'

'Mister,' rasped Jubal, 'right now the fanciest thing I feel like trying is a wrestling match with a pillow.'

He stood up and followed the rancher out of the office. Eli and Brandon came close behind. They crossed the main room and Jubal thought he heard a woman snivelling in one of the side chambers. Stoppard ignored the sounds, leading the way over to a narrow door that opened on a covered walkway. The outside wall was built up to the level of the roofs, but on the inside it opened onto the central courtyard. Stoppard opened the door at the far end and motioned Jubal inside.

'I'll send the tub,' he grunted, and chuckled. 'Make yourself at home.'

Jubal didn't bother replying.

The door snapped shut and the key clicked in the lock. There was the clatter of boot-heels on the tiled walkway; Jubal examined the room. It was a little larger than his earlier prison, and a whole lot more agreeable. The floor was polished timber with a thick woollen rug covering the centre. There was a wide bed with clean sheets and a mattress that – when he touched it – felt temptingly soft. A wardrobe occupied part of one wall, and there was an easy chair and a washstand. Windows were let into the centre of the inner and outer walls. He checked them, swinging the shutters back.

The outer window was covered with the fancy grille work he had seen coming in to the ranch. It bellied out enough that he could see a little way along the wall in both directions, but it was set firmly into the stone and the ornate pattern was too closely spaced to grant exit. He turned to the inner window.

Eli's face grinned slackly from the other side: as effective a barrier as the grille.

'Boss says you gotta stay in there,' smiled the giant. 'You just get comfortable an' don't start no trouble. I don't wanta hurt you no more.'

Jubal nodded and closed the shutters, fastening them in place.

He stripped out of his jacket and vest and shirt, then examined his damage in the mirror hinged atop the washstand. The yellowing of the facial bruise received from the two Fat W men was augmented by the spreading purple of new markings. One eye was blackened and his lips were swollen. His nose had bled, coating his jaw and neck with a brown crusting. One ear and the lines of his jaw were swollen, and his gums were cut. His arms were dark with the mottling of fists and kicks, and over his torso and back there was a patterning of red and purple. He stripped off the remainder of his clothes. Mostly, he had succeeded in protecting the more delicate parts of his body, but his legs and hips were badly bruised.

He began to flex his arms and bend his knees, testing for serious damage. He was horribly stiff, and it was painfully hard to raise his left arm, but so far as he could tell there was nothing broken. Riding would be a painful experience, and sudden movement was near-impossible, but he could still move. And his right arm was reasonably mobile. Maybe even enough for his purpose. He tugged a blanket from the bed and wrapped it around himself before slumping in the chair.

The door opened and Cole Brandon came in with the Winchester cocked. Jubal noted that the cowboy favoured the long gun even in the confines of the room.

'Just like a hotel, ain't it?' sneered Brandon. 'One bath, as ordered.'

He ducked his head and two men carried a steaming tub inside. Brandon stayed by the door, the carbine pointed at Jubal's chest, while they went to fetch buckets of cold water and towels. Then one tossed the medical valise onto the bed, and the other dropped a torn-up sheet on the washstand. Brandon chuckled and closed the door. The lock clicked again behind him.

Jubal let the blanket fall and climbed into the tub. The water was close to boiling. It stung the raw places on his body, but the heat seeped deep into his limbs and he lolled back with his eyes closed, letting the warmth ease his pain.

He was still not exactly sure how he would – could – implement the plan that had formed in his mind, but he had all the makings and so far things seemed to be falling into place.

He waited until the water was cooling, then soaped himself cautiously from head to foot and sluiced clean in the cold water. It was hard to lift the buckets, but the tingling chill made him feel better and also served to still the blood that was oozing from the cuts.

After drying himself he opened his bag and dressed the open wounds, then applied liniment to the bruises he could reach. When he was satisfied that he had done all he could to mend himself, he climbed under the sheets and went to sleep.

He woke briefly when the tub was removed and a plate of food set on the floor. He felt too weak to eat, so he left it there until he woke again. By then it was dark, and he had to open the outer shutters to check his watch. The gold Hunter told him he had slept the better part of twelve hours, so it was now well into the evening. He lifted the plate and examined the meal. Gravy had congealed around the steak, but the meat was still edible. He cut it into small pieces, chewing carefully. The potatoes were cold, but filling. He ignored the hardened biscuits. There was a mug of cold coffee that he drank for want of any other liquid, and then climbed back in bed and slept again.

The next time he woke it was soon after three in the morning. He shivered as he applied fresh medicaments to his wounds and bandaged himself.

He wrapped several strips of the sheeting around his ribs, cushioning the bruised areas, then reinforced his numb left arm with more. The dressings did little to ease the pain, but they cushioned the damaged areas against further harm.

It was past four by the time he was finished and the ranch was starting to wake up. A tracery of light came in through the shutters and a cock crowed somewhere outside, its strident challenge echoed by the yapping of a dog. He heard horses snicker as they were saddled, and the low-voiced muttering of sleepy cowhands.

He opened his valise and set his derby on the bed. From the medical bag, he selected a scalpel. It was short, small enough to conceal in the palm of his hand. The blade was curved, the upper edge blunt and straight. He used it to unpick part of the inner lining of the derby, then slotted the scalpel inside the envelope of loose material. Working fast in the dim light, he used a surgical needle and catgut to sew the cloth back in place. He left the stitches loose, ready to be broken.

When he was done, he put the derby back in the wardrobe and took a hypodermic from the valise. He cleansed the needle with alcohol from the small bottle inside the bag, and carefully measured a small dose of morphine into the plunger. He cleansed an area just below his left elbow with the alcohol and pinched a vein upright. Then he sank the needle into the bloodstream and eased the plunger down.

After that he cleaned the needle and set the hypodermic back in the bag. Then he climbed back into the bed and allowed the drug to take its effect.

He sank into a deep, dreamless sleep that was interrupted only by Cole Brandon.

The cowboy shook him awake, staring at Jubal's drowsy eyes and shaking his head in disbelief as the small man slid groggily from the bed. Brandon stayed with him as water was brought so that he could wash and shave, his angular frame leant back against the corner of the door with the carbine draped negligently in the crook of his left arm. Part of Jubal's mind watched through the haze of the drug-induced torpor, noting that Brandon had relaxed and aware that the cowboy's relaxation might afford him an advantage when the drug wore off. At least, when its immediate effects were dissipated.

'Figgered you'd be tougher,' murmured Brandon. 'I seen fellers hurt worse'n you on their feet the next day. You look like you'd fall off a rockin' chair.'

'I'll be all right.' Jubal's words were slurred. 'Don't worry.'

'You better,' said Brandon. 'We ride out inside the hour. Gonna take us two days to reach Gillard, the way you look.'

Jubal grunted and concentrated on dragging the razor over his cheeks.

When he was finished, he dusted his face with powder taken from the medical valise and worked ointment into the worst of the bruises. It was difficult to decide which were the worst, but the impromptu cosmetics served to mask the bruising some. Brandon passed him a clean shirt and he got dressed.

'Let's go,' said the cowboy. 'The boss wants to talk to you again.'

He prodded Jubal down the walkway to Stoppard's office.

The rancher was drinking coffee and smoking a cigar. He looked surprised when they came in, his scarred face frowning as Jubal swayed before him.

'Christ!' He set his coffee down. 'You look damn' awful. Can you make it?'

'Yeah,' mumbled Jubal. 'If we take it slow.'

'All right.' Stoppard nodded. 'You know what you gotta do?'

'Yeah.' The words were slow and thick through the dulling of the morphine. 'I know.'

'You better,' said Stoppard. 'Cole?'

'I know, boss.' Brandon grinned. 'Don't worry. Me an' Eli'll get him there on his feet. He'll tell Deke what you said.'

'You get any questions,' grunted the rancher, 'you tell Deke we found him like this after Wain's boys left him.'

'I got it, boss.' Brandon nodded. 'We'll be back inside four days.'

'Fine,' said Stoppard. 'Get him on a horse an' get him outta here. Fast.'

Jubal stumbled from the office into the outer room. Mary Stoppard looked at him from across the big table, the fork she was lifting to her mouth halted in mid-air. She set it down, shaking her head, and mumbled something he couldn't hear. Then Brandon had shoved him past, out onto the front porch.

Eli lifted him astride the bay pony and set his hands on the saddlehorn. Jubal realized that he felt even worse than he had planned to look: the morphine was dulling the pain as he had planned, and it had made his movements slow; shambling. But it was also dulling his mind. He hoped that effect would wear off as he had intended.

'Don't try nuthin', will you?' warned the giant. 'I don't wanta have to hurt you again.'

Jubal shook his head, clutching the saddlehorn as Eli led his pony away from the ranch buildings.

'Don't get the needle,' mumbled the big man. 'I'm just doing what I must.'

## CHAPTER TEN

They rode away from the Crazy Z with Eli leading Jubal's horse and Cole Brandon in the rear. Around late afternoon the worst effects of the morphine were gone and Jubal was able to think more clearly. Deliberately, he gave no sign of his recovery, continuing to sway in the saddle with his head down and shoulders rocking.

He kept up the pretence throughout what remained of the morning, and when they halted at noon, he let Eli lift him from the saddle. As the giant set him on the grass he folded his knees, collapsing on his face.

'Jesus! I seen chickens stronger'n him,' sneered Brandon. 'Pick him up, Eli.'

The man-mountain lifted Jubal like a baby and set him carefully on the grass. Brandon opened a can of beans and tossed it over. Jubal made an effort to catch the tin, hiding the anger that rose up when Brandon laughed as he dropped it. Eli retrieved it and handed it to him. He took the spoon the giant offered and ate slowly, making a deliberate show of clumsiness.

'Reckon you musta hit him too hard, Eli,' chuckled Brandon. 'Looks like his brain got fogged.'

'I'll be all right,' Jubal mumbled. 'You'll see.'

'I better,' said Brandon, his voice cold. 'You back out an' you're dead.'

'Best you do like Cole says,' added Eli. 'Then everythin' is fine an' we can take you where you want to go.'

Jubal said nothing. Just went on eating as the rage mounted inside him and threatened to boil over.

But not yet.

Not yet, he reminded himself. Not the right time. Wait.

Wait until it is right. Wait until the morphine has worn off and all it's doing is dulling the pain. Then move.

He emptied the can and let it fall to the grass. Brandon kicked it aside. 'Let's move. Sooner we get to Gillard, the sooner we get a drink.'

They rode on through the afternoon, cutting south down the long valley that held the heartland of Stoppard's spread before shifting eastwards to climb the flank of the ridge. The movement of the horse pained Jubal, but by now the shafts were dulled down to numb aches. The hot bath and the long sleep – most of all, the morphine – had reduced the bruising to a painful memory. The anger he felt pumped adrenalin into his blood stream, speeding his pulse rate and serving to dispel even farther the effects of the beatings. He tested his limbs as he rode, surreptitiously shifting his body until he was confident that he could carry out his plan.

Or at least attempt it.

But not yet. Not until dark, when the night might afford him some further advantage.

Meanwhile, he continued his pretence, swaying loose in the saddle as Eli led him up the slope towards the trees and Cole Brandon came behind, the carbine, Jubal noticed, in the saddle holster.

They moved clear of the grass and followed a narrow trail that wound along the side of the ridge, heading south. After a while it shifted up again, crossing the rimrock to devolve on the far side, where another valley folded southwards towards Gillard.

They crossed it, riding through thick masses of cattle fattening on the late summer grass, and began to mount the ridge beyond. The way got harder here, lifting up through folds of pine-clad rock and long sweeps of crumbled sandstone that slowed their passage with the intricacy of the miniature canyons and ravines. Jubal guessed that Brandon was choosing a deliberately slower path in order to allow him time to recover.

It fitted in with his original plan, and he fought to hide the grin threatening to break on his face. It wasn't difficult: smiling hurt his mouth and jaw.

They trailed up a bluff that ended on a small plateau ringed round with pines. The light was fading fast, the bottomlands already pooled into darkness and only the higher slopes still lit from the west. The sun was a big, red orb across to the far side of the horizon, and the light filling the clearing was pure gold cut through with the stark shadows of the pines.

'We'll sleep here,' Brandon announced. 'Ain't more'n a half day to Gillard, so we can give Cade some rest.'

Eli nodded and reined in.

Jubal lumped in the saddle, swaying slowly from side to side.

'Climb down,' said Brandon. 'We ain't goddam nursemaids.'

Jubal eased his right foot clear of the stirrup and swung it slowly across. He gritted his teeth as he let his left swing out and pitched flat on his back, tumbling over the grass that filled the hollow.

'Jesus!' moaned Brandon. 'He's like a goddam baby.'

Jubal got up on his hands and knees, shaking his head groggily. The grey derby had fallen from his head and he reached out to collect the hat, setting it carefully back in place. He maintained the charade of semi-consciousness as Eli dismounted and hauled him to a sitting position. By now the mind-dulling effects of the morphine were totally gone and the drug was beginning to lose its relaxing power over his hurts. The aches were starting to come back, and he could feel his body stiffening up again. Not badly, yet, but enough that he knew he had to make his play soon. He let his eyes go out of focus and his head loll down on his chest.

'You musta hit him a mite too hard, Eli.' Brandon seemed amused at the possibility. 'Looks like his brain got as addled as yourn.'

The giant shrugged, glancing nervously at the small man slumped on the grass.

'I never meant to hurt him that much, Cole.' He sounded almost apologetic. 'I was only doin' what I was told.'

'Yeah.' Brandon hobbled his horse and turned to face Jubal. He was now carrying the Winchester. 'You go right on doin' that, boy. Like now you can fix the horses an' then get us some wood fer a fire.'

Eli nodded and set to fixing hobbles on his own mount and Jubal's. Then he wandered off into the trees while Brandon sorted food from the saddlebags.

After a while Eli came back with a big armful of wood and set to preparing a meal. Brandon produced a bottle, tugging the cork with his teeth and taking a long swallow before passing it over to the giant.

'I'd offer you some,' he chuckled, 'but I don't reckon you're in no shape fer hard likker.'

Jubal said nothing.

When the food was ready, Eli passed him a plate. Jubal ate slowly: his mouth was starting to hurt again. The beans and fried jerky warmed his belly, though, and he felt he could sense the nourishment stoking the fires of hate inside him. He drank two cups of coffee, ignoring Brandon's laughter as the near-scalding liquid burned his gums.

The sun disappeared behind the western hills and the plateau got filled with shadow. The fire was a red-glowing beacon that accentuated the lean planes of Brandon's face, the slacker lines of Eli's. The two cowboys emptied half the bottle before Brandon hammered the cork home. He stood up.

'Gonna tie your hands and legs, feller. I don't want you tryin' nuthin' while we're asleep.'

Jubal grunted and thrust both arms out in front. Brandon wrapped a pigging string around his wrists, knotting it tight; did the same to Jubal's ankles. Eli dropped Jubal's saddle behind him and spread his bedroll on the ground. Jubal smiled slackly and stretched out. Eli swung the blanket to cover him.

He watched as the two cowboys prepared their own bedrolls. Cole Brandon set the Winchester down at the side of his, and Eli rested his shotgun on the saddle. Jubal nudged the grey derby down over his face and began to snore.

The fire dimmed, giving off only a dull, red glow that was complemented by the rising moon. A coyote howled, and a nightjar screamed. Somewhere off in the trees a squirrel chattered irritably, the sound rising to a shriek of defiance that ended abruptly as whatever predator had disturbed the animal's rest made its final pounce.

An owl drifted silently across the clearing.

Brandon began to snore.

Eli rolled on his side, one hand over the shotgun.

Jubal waited.

He waited until the moon was directly above the clearing and both cowboys were snuffing heavy breathing into the still air. The fire was no more than a pile of cinders, gleaming a faint red through the moonlit darkness. He reached slowly up to his face, lifting the hat away and settling it between his knees.

The loose-stitched sweat band came out easily, exposing the hidden scalpel. Jubal caught the handle in his fingers and set it between his boots. The pigging string holding his ankles together acted as a brace, and he used both feet to jam the thing steady as he began to saw the bonds around his wrists against the blade.

The honed metal sliced the string as easily as it would slice flesh: the cord parted in moments. Jubal flexed his fingers and massaged his wrists before cutting through the bindings on his ankles.

He stood up, still clutching the scalpel.

The Colt was holstered on his waist, but Brandon had emptied the chambers and stripped the belt of spare cartridges. The Spencer was similarly emptied. He didn't know if the cowboy had left the extra cartons of shells in his saddlebags; and didn't want to risk checking.

He realized that his plan had not been finalized. He had worked it out up to the escape – and so far it was working perfectly – but he had failed to envisage the problem of getting away without making any noise.

He picked up his saddle and carried it over to the bay horse.

The animal snickered sleepily as Jubal fastened the straps under its belly. He wondered if he should kill Brandon and Eli as they slept: decided against it, for it somehow offended his personal code to slaughter a sleeping – and thus defenceless – man.

He decided that he would take their horses with him. Lead them off to the north and then let them loose to find their own way back to the ranch. By the time the animals and the two men made their way back, he would be long gone to Blazeville.

Then the nightjar screamed again and Brandon woke up. His movement was purely instinctive: he set both hands on the Winchester and sat up, peering around the clearing.

The first thing he saw was Jubal, kneeling down to untie the hobble on his pony.

Reaction dictated his next move: he fired the carbine.

Brandon's horse screamed and collapsed onto its side with blood pumping from under its left shoulder.

Jubal spun round, legs bending into a crouch before he powered forwards. The scalpel was in his hand, blade gleaming briefly in the moonlight. Brandon's carbine detonated a second shot against the sky as Jubal's shoulder struck the barrel and deflected the cowboy's aim off into the empty night.

Jubal fastened one hand around the muzzle of the Winchester as he drove his left knee up into Brandon's groin. The cowboy gasped, spitting bile as the nausea thrust upwards through his intestines. Then the gasp ended. Abruptly. It ended with the slicing of the scalpel across his throat.

As Jubal kneed him, he doubled over, bringing his neck down onto the blade Jubal was lifting towards him. The scalpel lanced through the wind-weathered skin and cut deep into the muscle beneath. It sliced the cartilage and opened a gap into the pipes behind. Brandon felt the air in his lungs empty uselessly into the night. At the same time a thick spray of blood fountained high into the air.

Jubal rolled aside, dragging back the man's head so that the wound was opened even wider. Brandon choked on the gore filling his throat. His body convulsed, knees lifting up against his chest and then slamming back against the grass as his heels dug deep into the turf and his spine arced so that he was spread like a strung bow: only heels and head touching the ground.

Jubal dragged the scalpel back from the gaping wound in the neck and drove it across and over the body. The point went in under Cole Brandon's lower ribs, cutting with surgical precision into the heart. It sliced through the right ventricle, spilling a massive surge of blood out from the tortured organ so that the flow of oxygen to the brain was cut off and the man gargled and died with fountains of crimson dancing darkly in the moon's light from his throat and chest.

The scalpel grated against a rib, the indentation between blade and handle catching on the bone as the cowboy jerked and died. Jubal let it go, rolling clear of the writhing corpse to fetch up on his feet with his eyes fixed on his horse.

Eli woke up.

'What? What is it?'

He began to cock the scattergun.

Jubal kicked him in the chest, tumbling him back over his saddle. The giant shook his head and brought the shotgun round to his chest, oblivious of the kick.

Jubal stamped on the barrel, then brought his other foot down hard over Eli's wrist. The shotgun blasted a long, wide channel through the grass. Eli screamed as his wrist was snapped. There was the dull sound of breaking bones and the stink of scorched grass. Eli let the shotgun fall as blood-covered shards of splintered bone tore upwards through his hand.

Jubal kicked him again, landing the point of his boot clean against the giant's chin. Eli's head snapped back, teeth closing on the tongue so that a sliver of pink fell from between his lips.

Jubal turned and ran for his horse. He felt no regrets about killing Cole Brandon, but Eli was somehow different. The man was like a child: an overly powerful idiot, with no more responsibility for his actions than a gun. He was a tool, used by people like Laz Stoppard and Cole Brandon to further their own aims.

Jubal didn't want to kill Eli. Not unless he was forced to.

'Can't let you go. Gotta do what the boss said.'

Jubal felt himself hauled from the bay pony as Eli's massive arms closed around his waist.

One hand was hanging free, blood spilling over the fingers and palm while splinters of pale bone stuck up through the skin. Jubal groaned, feeling his breath sucked clear of his lungs and a relentless pressure closing tight about his midriff. He felt his heart pound, felt the old bruises give way to the new pain. Blood drummed in his ears. He thought his ribs were breaking.

He reached back, fastening his hands on Eli's ears. The giant went on squeezing as Jubal traced a line from the ears across the temples, down to the face. His mouth opened wide and the moon got red before he found what he wanted.

By then he was almost crushed to death, but he still managed to fasten both hands into fists. With the thumbs jutting out.

And drive both thumbs back into Eli's eyes.

The giant screamed. Jubal felt soft pulp gout over his hands. Felt his knuckles jar on the ridges of bone inside the eye sockets.

And then was dropped free.

He fell onto the grass and launched himself away from the stumbling, screaming giant. Eli was still on his feet, both hands pressed against the pits of his eyes, blood and a thick pulsing of fluid spouting from between his fingers.

Jubal gagged, moving over to his horse.

He got into the saddle and turned the animal south. Eli stumbled towards him, hands lifted out to expose the bleeding holes in his face.

'No!' he shouted. 'I can't let you go. I gotta do what I was told.'

Jubal dug his heels into the bay pony's flanks and powered the horse forwards.

It hit Eli and spun him round. Somehow he kept his balance,

stumbling over the clearing with both arms still reaching for his duty. He managed to fasten a hand on the bridle, dragging the pony's head down.

'Let go!' Jubal yelled. 'For God's sake, let go!'

Eli just spat blood and went on hanging on the reins.

The bay panicked. It went back on its hindquarters and pawed the air.

The hooves came down onto Eli's skull.

Bone split, gouting crimson and grey brain matter through the moonlit air. Eli grunted and fell away from the horse, stumbling back towards the perimeter of the trees.

The pony went on bucking, screaming its panic. Jubal felt his own fear contort his face into a mask of rage. He felt his skin get tight as hate and anger took hold, stretching his cheeks out so that the scar tissue over his nose shone white in the pale moonlight. His nostrils flared and his lips compressed into a taut line. He groaned an inarticulate cry and launched the bay pony straight at Eli.

The giant fell down under the hooves. The bay hit him on the run, then got tugged back by Jubal so that the hooves pounded down onto the cowboy's body, sharding ribs and legs and arms.

Eli was mashed as Jubal danced the horse round and round over his corpse.

When the rage faded, Jubal walked the pony over to the far side of the plateau.

He felt sick. With himself and with life. He looked at the mangled body and shook his head.

'Sorry, Eli,' he murmured, 'but there's some things a man just can't ride around.'

Eli never heard that one, either.

## CHAPTER ELEVEN

Jubal paused, listening to the night. The surrounding trees had muffled the detonations of Brandon's Winchester and Eli's shotgun, and there was no hint of approaching danger. He checked his saddlebags and found the cartons of shells still there. Reloading the Colt and the Spencer, he assessed his position.

Brand had said they were a half day from Gillard. That put him at least two days away from Blazeville, most of the distance over Stoppard land. The supplies he had purchased were gone and the struggle with Eli reminded him how weak he was. The last effects of the morphine were totally dissipated now, and the giant's crushing grip had used up the last reserves of his energy. He thought a rib might be broken. Knew that he was incapable of staying in the saddle for long, certainly not long enough to traverse the Crazy Z safely.

He wondered what to do, trying to force a degree of coherent thought into a mind confused by pain and the after effects of the drug.

Two thoughts came to him. The first was that Mary Wilson had appeared friendly and knew something about doctoring. The second was that with two of Stoppard's men dead he was in trouble with both the big ranches.

He forced himself to reason clearly.

After killing two Fat W hands, it seemed unlikely that Jason Wain or anyone else would expect him to return to Gillard. Stoppard knew that he wanted to get to Blazeville, so it was logical that the rancher would seek him in that direction.

And there was another consideration. He had never sought to become involved in the power struggle for the Last homestead: he had been dragged into it unwilling. But now – as Stoppard had said – he was involved. Not for any personal reward, nor for any personal interest in the final outcome of the struggle. But he had suffered a beating at the hands of men from the Fat W, and more from the Crazy Z. And that angered him. Prompted him to apply his own brand of justice to the situation, and the best way to do that seemed to be by warning Jane Last of Stoppard's intentions.

Besides, he felt too weak to make the journey to Blazeville.

He dug his heels against the flanks of the bay pony and guided the animal clear of the plateau.

Most of the journey south got lost in a wavering mist of pain that threatened to spill him clear of the saddle and leave him bait for the kites and buzzards he saw circling as the sun came up. By then he could see Gillard. The town was beginning to come to life. Smoke was getting thicker from the stacks as breakfast got cooked, and a few early risers were moving about the streets. Not many, but enough that he began to worry about getting in unseen.

There was a stand of cottonwood just outside the town with a thin trickle of water running through the centre. It was around a quarter mile away and the ground between was open grass. He rode the bay pony in amongst the trees and eased down from the saddle. His knees were shaking and it took him a long time to haul the saddle clear and tether the pony. He fastened it on a rope long enough that it could crop the grass inside the trees, and then lifted the medical bag and the Spencer and began to walk towards Gillard.

It was one of the longest walks of his life. His feet felt like lead lumps on the ends of limbs that he couldn't control properly. The lowing of the cattle on the long downward slope sounded like the murmur of the sea, beating against his confused mind in pounding waves that threatened to overwhelm him. The grass shimmered in the early sunlight, distorting his vision so that he peered, blinking tears, through a flickering curtain of green and gold. The first time he fell down he pushed upright on hands and knees. The second time, he used the

Spencer as a crutch. The next few times he crawled forwards until he felt strong enough to walk again, tottering on like a man too drunk to handle himself.

He reached the rear of Gillard and slumped heavily against a paling fence. A dog barked at him and he stumbled on into the shadows of the adjoining alley. The air was cool with the early morning chill and he found himself shivering, sweat cooling too fast on his face and body. He stared around, fighting to recall the location of Mary Wilson's house.

He found it and kicked the gate open. The flowers were still fighting to survive and the apple tree looked as withered as ever, but someone had walked a horse over the garden and pumped bullets into the tree. He went up to the door and tapped the frame.

Mary Wilson opened the door, looking like her garden: old and tired and threatened.

'My God!' Her bird-bright eyes flickered over his face. 'You came back.'

'I need help.' The words came out thick and slurred. 'Got to hide.'

She pushed the door back with her cane and beckoned him inside.

'Who did that to you? Jason's men?'

'No.' Jubal shook his head slowly. 'Stoppard's.'

The old woman closed the door. 'Laz Stoppard ain't like that. He never made trouble before.'

'I guess he never thought he could buy the Last place before,' mumbled Jubal. And slid down the wall onto the threadbare carpet.

He began to cough, and realized that Mary Wilson was holding a bottle of smelling salts under his nose. He blinked, pushing the bottle away as the ammonia salts cleared his head.

'I followed the trail you told me, only Stoppard's men took me in.' He climbed to his feet, helped by the old woman. 'Then they beat me up.'

He explained what had happened as Mary Wilson helped

him into the living room and settled him on a horse-hair sofa.

'Goddamit!' she muttered. 'I got troubles enough already, without you addin' to them. Jason's men already messed my garden, an' Jane's about ready to have the kid.'

'Sorry,' mumbled Jubal. 'I never wanted to come here.'

'Yeah.' The old woman got businesslike. 'You just wanted to get to Blazeville. Now you want to get to bed. For a long time, judgin' by the look of you.'

'Can you hide me?' Jubal asked. 'I didn't know where else to go.'

She tutted some, but when she looked at his face again she was smiling.

'Sure I'll hide you. Don't reckon anyone'll think of lookin' fer you here. Besides, I got a kinda sneakin' respect for anyone ready to stand up against Jason an' Laz both.'

'Thanks.' Jubal let her help him to his feet, draping one arm around her shoulders as she walked him into one of the rear rooms.

It was clean and cool and quiet. Chintz curtains covered the windows and there was a smell of camphor in the air. The slanting rays of the early sun angled over the bed at the centre. Mary Wilson pulled back the embroidered coverlet to expose white sheets and a mound of fresh-looking pillows.

'I'll fetch some water,' she said. 'You get yoreself in there.'

Jubal remembered to shove his Colt under the pillows and prop the Spencer against the wall beside him before he closed his eyes and gave way to the black vortex sucking on his mind.

He slept long and deep and sound, waking to darkness and the odour of cooking. He smelled something frying and realized that he was hungry, but then sleep took him again and he rolled over, burying his head in the pillows and giving himself back to the welcome darkness.

The next time it was light and Mary Wilson was perched on the bed with a mug in her hands.

'Broth. Drink it.'

He let her help him, savouring the rich taste even though it hurt his mashed mouth. When he was finished she brought him a second mug and he sat up, running a hand over his jaw. It was still swollen, but now the bruises were covered with the stubbly overlay of several days' beard growth.

'How long?' he asked.

The old woman chuckled. 'They usually ask "Where am I?". Mighta known you'd be different. Three days.'

He was surprised. He had no sense of passing time and this sun-filled afternoon might as well have been the first day. He asked about his horse, worried at leaving the animal so long untended.

'Don't worry,' said the old woman. 'I listened to you long enough to find out where you left it. Still there, only I been feedin' it every day. Folks round here are used to me wanderin' off to look for herbs, so I had a pretty good excuse to carry a basket full of oats out. What you give yourself?'

Instinctively, Jubal glanced down at his arm. Where he had injected the morphine, his flesh was bruised, an ugly red circle surrounding the point of the injection.

'Morphine,' he said. 'I needed something to dull the pain.'

'Yeah.' She sounded disapproving. 'I guess you had to do that. I been feedin' you herbs since – natural remedies are the best. Them an' plenty of sleep. Few more days an' you'll be fit to make that ride up to Blazeville. If you still want to go.'

There was something about her voice that warned Jubal his delayed journey would take longer still.

'What's happened?' he asked. 'You had trouble?'

'Not me so much as Jane,' said the old woman. 'I done everything I could for her, but the baby was born dead.'

'Oh, hell,' Jubal said. 'I'm sorry.'

'You done everything you could,' said Mary Wilson. 'More'n most folks around here. I guess it simplifies things, though I'm not lookin' forward to that.'

'What do you mean?' Jubal stared at the lined face, conscious of some ulterior motive. 'I don't understand.'

'It's easy,' said the midwife. 'Jane is still Jason's daughter, so he's got prior claim on that land. Gil's folk back East might try to muscle in, but there ain't a court in the West that'll uphold their claim, so it gets left with Jason. Laz Stoppard'll try to buy it – like you told me he was plannin' to do – but Jason ain't gonna take that.'

Jubal drank more broth and asked, 'What are you trying to tell me?'

'Gillard gets hit,' she said. 'Whichever way you look at it. Hell! Gil Last stirred up more trouble than he knew how to handle. He set Laz an' Jason so deep into one another's throats that they can't forget it now. If Jason gets the land, Laz'll be startin' a range war. If Laz buys it, then Jason'll be fighting to take it over. Either way a whole lotta decent people get hurted.'

'What's that to do with me?' Jubal asked. 'I never wanted to get involved.'

'Nor'd I,' said Mary Wilson. 'I wish you'd never found Gil. Never brought Jane in here. But you did. I guess that's the way it goes sometimes: you just pick up responsibilities without meaning to.'

Like Andy, Jubal thought. Or trying to find the man who killed your wife.

'All right,' he said, accepting. 'What can I do?'

'I thought you was headin' fer Blazeville,' said Mary Wilson, her tired face splitting partway to a smile. 'Had a man to find up there.'

'I guess I owe you,' Jubal acknowledged. 'Maybe I'll hang around.'

'Be exactly what'll you do if Jason or Laz find you,' said the midwife. 'I was kinda hopin' you'd have ideas of your own.'

Jubal shrugged, suddenly aware that his body didn't hurt so much. He was still stiff. Could still feel the bruises. But now he felt capable of moving. Of action.

And an idea was forming.

'The baby died?' he asked. 'But the mother's all right?'

Mary Wilson nodded. 'Sure. Like I said.'

'Who knows?'

'Me. Jane. You. I wasn't exactly spreading word on what happened.'

'And Jane's here now?'

The midwife nodded. 'Sure. Been helpin' me tend you. Gave her something to do. Something to take her mind off it.'

'And the baby?' he asked. 'Where's that?'

'*Him*,' the old lady replied. 'Was a boy child. I wrapped him up and got him ready fer burial. Circuit preacher don't come by here more'n once a month.'

'And there's no one else knows?'

She shook her head. 'No one. I din't want Jane troubled by well-wishers. Or the bastards who wish her ill.'

'Good.' Jubal smiled, exposing his broken teeth. 'That's good.'

'I don't follow you, son.' Mary Wilson frowned, adding a fresh set of wrinkles to her face. 'What you talkin' about?'

'Who'd back her?' Jubal asked, ignoring the question. 'Is there any in Gillard would come out to support her?'

Mary Wilson thought about it for less than a minute before she said, 'No. Ain't no one.'

'Marshal Tago?' Jubal queried. 'What about him?'

'Deke?' She made the name sound like spitting. 'He just wants to feed his face an' stay the right side of everyone.'

'The banker?' said Jubal. 'Carter?'

'Ole Henry? He'd be a bounty man if'n he weren't too fat an' old to use a gun.'

'They hang to either side?' Jubal asked. 'They favour one ranch more than the other?'

Mary Wilson snorted. 'Men like that get sore asses from sittin' on the fence. Only way they keep their balance is bobbin' from side to side to see who's lookin'. They'd be scared to put a foot down either side.'

'That's good,' Jubal said, emptying his bowl. 'That suits us.'

'I guess you're tryin' to help,' said Mary Wilson. 'But I don't understand how.'

'There's more than one way to skin a cat,' Jubal grinned. 'And a baby looks much the same.'

'I don't follow you,' said the old lady. 'I don't understand.'

'You will,' Jubal replied. 'When we peel the hide off.'

## CHAPTER TWELVE

It was three days later before Jubal felt well enough to move. Jane Last was already moving about the house, and Mary Wilson was fretting over the delay.

On the fourth day the midwife fetched the wagon from the stable along with the dog. On Jubal's suggestion she told Billy Judge that Jane could no longer afford stable fees, so she was taking the wagon back to the Last homestead, where all the animals could fend for themselves.

She took it out early in the morning, gathering a few of her own possessions from the clapboard house before riding it round to the back, where Jane clambered on board. By then Jubal had already collected his horse and was waiting for them in the cottonwood stand.

He waited until the wagon was gone clear up the ridge before following after. It was early in the morning and so there were few people watching their departure. The wagon climbed the slope easily, Mary Wilson handling the two-horse team like a trained skinner. Jubal followed behind like a shadow.

They took it slowly, following the narrow trail that ran along the crest of the ridge through the treeline before cutting down-slope to the north-east. The ground was hard enough that no tracks would show, though Jubal guessed that Billy Judge would spread word before long, and that both the ranchers would send men out to check the homestead. By the time they arrived he hoped to be ready for them.

Twice, they halted inside timber breaks, watching as cowboys crossed their path through the pasture lands below.

'Most like they're lookin' fer you,' remarked Mary Wilson. 'That goddam gossip at the stable told me how they found two bodies up on the west rise. Guess they'd be the fellers you killed.'

'I guess.' Jubal mouthed a silent curse: he had hoped it would take longer to find Brandon and Eli. The early discovery cut down his time. 'He say anything else?'

'Only that Laz Stoppard was almighty angry,' grinned the old woman. 'But we figgered on that, anyway.'

'*We?*' Jubal asked. 'You don't have to stay in this. Just get us up to the Last place and then you can go back home. They won't do anything to you.'

'Because I'm too old?' she chuckled. 'Don't you count on it, son. Them greedy bastards know I was tendin' Jane, an' they still think the baby's alive. So long as they go on thinkin' that I'm in deep. Besides, I want to see what happens.'

'It'll be dangerous,' Jubal warned. 'They're not about to take kindly to anyone helping me.'

'Nor Jane.' The old woman ducked her head at the younger female. 'An' she still needs a woman's care.'

Jubal shrugged; agreeing. Jane Last was slumped on the seat of the wagon with a black shawl dragged tight around her shoulders despite the mounting heat. Her hair was lank, tugged back from her face in a single long tail. The arrangement served to accentuate the waxy pallor of her skin, emphasizing the lines around her eyes and mouth. There were deep shadows beneath both eye sockets and she nibbled incessantly on her lower lip. The dark blue dress she wore was spread wide between her legs, forming a sling for the small tin resting there. Her hands stroked constantly over the surface, touching the lid and sides as though seeking reassurance.

It was an old biscuit tin, the lettering long rubbed away so that the dull silver metal was exposed. The lid was sealed to the body with pitch.

'How long?' Jubal asked. 'Before we get there?'

'Sundown.' Mary Wilson urged the horses forward. 'Maybe just before.'

They took a different trail to the one Jubal had followed,

cutting up through a narrow valley and skirting around the flank of a rise before they entered the high meadow containing the Last homestead. The sun was fading away behind the western ridge, filling the vee-shape of the meadow with a rich golden light. The twin streams flowing either side of the cabin were moving faster than Jubal remembered, the rush of water drowning out the clopping of the horses' hooves.

The dog raced on ahead, starting as he crossed the meadow. Jubal cocked the Spencer and followed.

The hooves of the bay pony began to make squelching sounds, and Jubal saw that the shimmer on the grass was the result of overspilled water. He looked towards the dams Gil Last had built, and saw that they were torn down, thus allowing the penned water to spill across the grass.

When he reached the cabin it was quiet and dark. The dog whined at the door and then ran round to the corral, where it began to bark.

Jubal slid to the ground, angling the Spencer into the dying light.

Something large was shadowed over by the fence. When he got closer, he saw that it was the corpse of the plough horse, and spat as the stink hit his nostrils. Buzzards and coyotes had opened up the animal's belly and there was a spread of entrails falling from the hole. The right side of the skull was pounded in by bullets and busy ants were making the most of the fading daylight as they scurried over the neck and flank.

The rough marker on Gil Last's grave was stamped down.

Jubal waved the wagon in.

'We gotta bury him.' Jane Last's voice was dull as her eyes. 'I promised him that.'

She climbed down from the wagon and carried the biscuit tin over to her husband's grave. Began to scoop at the earth with her hands.

Mary Wilson hitched the team to the fence and moved to haul the woman back.

'We'll do it, honey. We'll do it, Jane. Don't worry.'

She looked at Jubal as the widow began to cry, her old eyes framing a question. Jubal nodded and fetched the same shovel he had used to dig Gil Last's final resting place from the outhouse. He began to turn dirt.

It didn't take long: the tin holding Jane Last's baby wasn't very big.

There was still light in the sky when he finished and stamped the earth down over the small hole. He set Gil's cross upright again and fashioned a second for the child. The mother went on weeping, silently; and Mary Wilson began to intone a prayer.

The dog whined quietly and the sun went down, leaving the valley in darkness.

Jubal opened the cabin, surprised to find it undamaged. He lit the lamps and got the fire started in the stove. Set a pot of coffee to boiling on the top. After a while, Mary Wilson came in with her arms around Jane.

'I'll fix a bed,' she said. 'An' get us a meal. You want to do somethin' about that dead horse?'

Jubal nodded and went back into the night. The big dog followed him, growling irritably as a coyote yapped from across the valley. He found a sack of lye in the outhouse and emptied the contents over the body. Then he brought the bay pony and the wagon horses inside the corral and fed them oats from the sacks piled behind the house. He carried the sack over to the far side of the corral, as far as possible from the corpse.

When he returned to the cabin Mary Wilson was preparing food.

'Jane's asleep,' she said. 'How d'you feel?'

For the first time that day Jubal became aware of his bruises. There was nothing major troubling him, but his whole body seemed possessed by one massive ache. He filled a tin mug with coffee and settled into a chair.

'Not too bad.' He sipped the coffee cautiously. 'You?'

'Curious,' said Mary Wilson. 'What exactly d'you figger to gain by comin' back here?'

'Easy.' Jubal remembered the whisky Gil Last had been

carrying. He found the bottle where he had left it and topped his coffee. 'A deal between Stoppard and Wain. They both want this place, only now neither one's got any advantage.'

'Except the first one to ride in an' kill us all gets to own it,' grunted the midwife. 'Seems to me like you set us down twixt skillet an' pan.'

Jubal shook his head, savouring the food smells filling the cabin. 'No. Like you said: neither one of them can afford to start a range war. Laz Stoppard told me he needs this water for his winter grazing.'

The old lady nodded, forking meat and greens onto two plates.

'Sure he does. So does Jason. That still leaves us sittin' in the middle.'

'Stoppard said Wain couldn't afford to buy. That right?'

She passed him his plate and shrugged. 'Could be. I ain't exactly privvy to all their secrets, but I reckon Jason extended hisself a mite too far when he went into lumber.'

'So he can't afford to buy Jane out,' Jubal said, between mouthfuls. 'Stoppard can. Only he's got to have her name on the documents, or he gets into a war he can't afford.'

'Maybe.' She sat down facing him, chewing slowly on the meat. Then she spluttered and turned her head aside, fiddling with her mouth. When she turned back her lips were shrunk and there was something in her hand. 'Goddam teeth! I never shoulda bought them. Go on.'

'Stoppard thought to fix the deal by having me sign those papers,' Jubal said. 'He thought that would give him the chance to phase Wain out. All legal.'

'Only now he can't.' Mary Wilson gummed her food slowly. 'That still leaves both of 'em mad at you. An' both wantin' this place.'

'Sure.' Jubal grinned and poured more whisky. 'Only now they're both on an equal footing.'

'So why shouldn't one o' them send a few good old boys in to shoot the hell out of us?' She spat a strand of gristle onto her plate. 'Just kill us all an' claim water rights?'

'Billy Judge knew we were coming up here, didn't he?' Jubal spooned up the last of his gravy. 'And Billy Judge has a big mouth?'

'You should know, son. Was Billy passed the word to Joe Farmer an' Norm Clayton. Reason you got beat up.'

'So he'll be passing it again,' grinned Jubal. 'To anyone cares to listen. By now I reckon Deke Tago knows about where we are. And Henry Carter.'

'What good's that do us?' Mary Wilson frowned. 'All Deke wants is a quiet life. All Henry wants is profit.'

'This place is inside Tago's jurisdiction, isn't it?'

She nodded. 'Sure it is. Inside the county line.'

'So he's answerable for any killings that happen?' Jubal poured more coffee. Added a measure of whisky. 'Be questions asked if a widow lady got murdered on her own property?'

'I guess.' Mary Wilson began to smile: realizing what he was getting at. 'Yeah! There would. Be a Federal Marshal come lookin' around.'

'And Henry Carter can't sell a place that's occupied by the owner's widow?'

'No.' She shook her head, the smile getting wide enough to expose her gums. She gasped, and set the false teeth back in her mouth. Her voice got clear again. 'O' course he can't. He needs Jane's signature. Or his bank starts asking questions.'

'So we got insurance,' said Jubal. 'Anyone tries to shoot us up, they have a Federal Marshal checking things out. Or some Eastern bank. And in between, they start a range war they can't afford.'

'You think they'll realize that?' The old lady picked up the dishes and carried them over to the sink. 'You think they're that bright?'

'They have to see it,' said Jubal; hoping he was right. 'Stoppard will. And Jason Wain must know what could happen. If he didn't, he'd have taken this spread long ago. Before Stoppard moved in.'

'You're sneaky,' said Mary Wilson. 'Real sneaky. I like that. Feller like you could go a long way.'

'Fifty miles is all I want,' grunted Jubal. 'As far as Blazeville.'

'When you fixin' to leave?' she asked. 'I don't aim to stay up here the rest o' my life.'

Jubal shrugged. 'Jane decides that. Soon as she's well enough to make sensible decisions she's got some to make.'

'Like what?' asked Mary Wilson.

'Way I see it,' Jubal said, 'is she's got about four choices. She can stay on here and keep the spread going. Or she can just up and quit.'

'Don't see how she'd manage either,' interrupted the old lady. 'She can't run this place on her own, an' there ain't no one around these parts gonna risk buckin' the Fat W or the Crazy Z. Wouldn't be worth their lives. But if she quits, then she don't have nothin'. What's the other two?'

'She auctions the place off,' said Jubal. 'Sets it up like Laz Stoppard wants.'

'That means Laz gets it,' said Mary, her face creasing up into an irritable frown. 'Means the war starts anyway, an' Gillard suffers.'

'Fourth way is hard,' murmured Jubal. 'It'll take doing. Maybe more killing.'

'Jesus!' The old lady clashed her false teeth together. 'When I said you was sneaky, I was wrong. You're goddam devious.'

Jubal shrugged. 'Might be best in the long run. Depends if you want a range war, or not. All I want is to get away. Alive.'

'Tell me.' She began to wash the dishes. 'What you got figgered out in that cunnin' little mind?'

'We set up a meeting,' Jubal said. 'Between Laz Stoppard and Jason Wain. They buy Jane out between them – or she chooses to stay on. Either way, they both sign papers to guarantee they won't foul up the water. That way there's no war and Jane gets whatever she wants.'

'I didn't think I was that far wrong,' grinned Mary Wilson. 'But you're not even devious. You're worse: you're goddam brilliant. When do we do it?'

'After they've both calmed down,' said Jubal. 'And after we've all got some rest.'

The old lady chuckled: 'I'll fix you a bed.'

'Thanks,' said Jubal. 'I'll go check outside.'

He picked up the Spencer and stepped out onto the porch. The dog left the bone it was gnawing and went with him. Outside, the night was clear and cold. The lye had quashed the stink of the decomposing horse and a breeze was taking the sharp odour of the chemical away from the cabin. The moon was up, scudding behind an overlay of dark cloud that presaged the colder weather to come, its fullness melted down as it waned.

Jubal held the Spencer crooked in his left arm as he made a circuit around the cabin. There was no sign of danger, nor any sound other than the gurgling of the two streams and the natural noises of the night. He checked the horses in the corral and then returned to the porch, where he lit a cheroot.

He drew the aromatic smoke deep into his lungs and let it out in a long, slow sigh. The dog wagged its tail and settled on its hindquarters, tongue lolling out and eyes staring darkly up at his face. Absently, he reached down to scratch the heavy neck. The dog stretched, emitting a gusting sigh, and eased down on all fours. Jubal crouched beside it, drawing on the cheroot and rubbing the coarse hair of the beast's shoulders. The dog licked his hand.

Up on the eastern rise, where the moonlight shone brightest, a whipoorwill called. Off to the north a coyote bayed a lonesome cry. The two rivers went on tumbling the soft sounds of running water into the night and an owl let loose a single hollow hoot.

Jubal listened to the sounds, enjoying the cheroot and the

friendship of the big dog. He thought about the home he had planned to build. Once. A long time ago.

A long time ago when he had a new bride and high hopes. When he was eager to start a medical practice in the West. Where doctors were needed, because men were building a new frontier that involved bullets along with the building and they needed trained doctors to tend them. To answer the ravages of the frontier with skills learned just as hard in the softer climate of the East.

Now he had learned the other skills. Those of killing. Of hate, and its application. Had learned to shoot without compunction. And learned that such violence answered a deep call within his soul that took pleasure from the action.

He wanted to get to Blazeville.

Wanted to find the man called Lee Kincaid who had killed his wife.

And at the same time knew that he wanted to confront Laz Stoppard and Jason Wain for what they had done to him. Wanted to call them out into the open. Out from behind their façades of respectability and money, and so present to them the raw argument of the gun. To set them both in a position where only personal skill and courage mattered. Out where the teeth were bared and only killing power counted. Out to where lawyers and bankers and marshals had no meaning: only a man's personal ability to hate and survive.

He touched the Spencer, wondering idly how many men it had killed.

Wondering how many more there would be.

The cheroot burned down against his fingers and he tossed it out over the damp grass, watching the tiny pinprick of light sizzle into darkness. Like a glow-worm dying. Like a life fading away.

The dog rested its head on his thigh. He scratched its ears, thinking about times past. Thinking about a future he almost regretted.

Then he stood up.

The dog whined as he began to close the cabin door, pawing at the timber.

'Sorry,' said Jubal. 'But there's always one of us has to stay outside.'

# CHAPTER THIRTEEN

Sometime during the night a squall blew up, lashing rain against the shuttered windows and sending a fug of smoke back from the fireplace. Jubal woke from a dreamless sleep with one hand stretching automatically for the Spencer. The carbine was fisted up, the muzzle angled at the door, before he was fully aware of his surroundings. He recognized the sound of the rain and yawned. Pale grey light was filtering into the room and when he glanced at his watch, he saw that it was just short of five. He pushed the blanket aside and rose from the sofa, shivering in the early cold.

Shucking into his jacket, he opened the door. The big dog barked, shaking a spray of moisture from its coat as it darted inside. Jubal peered into the rain. The far side of the ridge was obscured behind the downpour, but the early light was bright enough that he could see the clouds scudding overhead, driven westwards by the wind. He swung the door shut and blew the stove into fresh life. There was still coffee in the pot, and he set it to heating while he cleaned up.

He was shaving when Mary Wilson came into the room. She was fully dressed, but her face was further aged by worry and a bad night's sleep.

'Gettin' too goddam old fer this kinda escapade,' she grumbled. 'Don't sleep right in a strange bed.'

Jubal grinned and passed a mug of coffee. She took a sip and pulled a face.

'Horse piss! Never did know a man could make decent coffee. Get out the way an' I'll brew us some fresh.'

'I'll check the horses.' He pulled on his stormcoat and went out into the dawn. The dog came with him, its huge paws splashing over the wet grass. The animal seemed to have taken a liking to him, or maybe it was just that it was accustomed to having a man around the place. He wondered what would happen to it if Jane Last decided to sell the homestead. Then realized he was jumping too far ahead and corrected his thoughts – if she lived long enough to sell the place.

He found the horses sheltering in the lean-to and forked fresh oats into the manger. The sky was beginning to clear, the rain drifting away to the west. The line of the valley's eastern edge was already bathed in light, the sky above tinging pink as the sun rose. He wondered how long it would take the ranchers to make their first move.

And then a fresh doubt crossed his mind as he remembered the mysterious gunman who had stopped him before. The man was an unknown factor, his obvious interest in the Last homestead an unexplained facet of the problem.

Back in the cabin he asked Mary Wilson about the man, but she just shook her head and denied any knowledge of him. Jubal decided to face whatever problems the man might present when they arose. For now he had enough on his mind worrying about Laz Stoppard and Jason Wain and Jane Last.

The woman, at least, was a minor worry. The loss of both her husband and child seemed to have left her numbed. Physically, she was recovering well: whatever herbal brews Mary Wilson was feeding her appeared to be rebuilding her reserves of energy. But emotionally, she seemed drained. Her movements were those of a sleepwalker, carried out with a dreamy slowness and a total lack of interest in her surroundings. She allowed Mary to set food before her, but had to be reminded before she ate it. She ignored the dog that nudged her with its massive head and whined for attention. And she seemed not to see Jubal at all. The only thing that awoke any spark of interest in her was the double grave outside the cabin. As soon as it was full light, she drew a shawl around her shoulders and went outside. When Jubal followed, he found her squatting by the graves, staring at the two crosses.

'She'll pull out of it,' said Mary Wilson. 'I seen folks took that way afore. Give her time an' she'll come back. That's what she needs – time.'

Jubal wondered if that was right. The worm of hate that had been planted in his own soul by the killing of his wife still had its fangs buried deep. He had learned to live with it just as a man might learn to live with a crippled leg. But learning to live with loss or hate didn't mean learning to accept it. For his own part, he realized that the worm could only be exorcized by the death of Lee Kincaid. And even that wouldn't bring Mary back. He recognized that her murder had changed him irrevocably. Had transformed him from a dedicated student of medicine to a man bent on revenge. His initial purpose, when he returned from his studies in England, had been to start a medical practice in the West. Where good doctors were needed. Now that purpose was transformed, as though a coin had been flipped, to the relentless pursuit of personal vengeance.

That alteration of original purpose had changed his personality, his way of thinking. This sojourn in the valley was, to him, merely a way-stop along his road. He still planned to get to Blazeville, and the only reason he had chosen to stay over to help Jane Last was because the men who had wronged her had wronged him, too. It was the kind of reasoning he had slowly adopted since Mary's death: the cold logic that dictated he leave no enemies behind him. At least, none alive.

He spent the morning checking the valley. The Lasts' few cattle were grazing contentedly on the rich grass at the northern end. There was a spread of ploughed ground that might once have grown wheat or corn, but it had been trampled, the fences broken down and the cattle allowed in. Both dams were torn down. The damage Jubal had seen riding in with the two women became clear as he studied the ruined workings. Gil Last had put a lot of misguided effort into building his dams. Had died for it. And now they were just loose piles of timber and earth; months of felling trees and carting the trunks down to the water, months of spading soil and chinking gaps, months of digging side channels, were all gone.

It looked as though blasting powder had been used to open the main barriers, and then the splintered timbers had been hauled clear by rope teams. The end result was a litter of water-logged, splintered wood and two clear-running streams.

Jubal recognized the debris as the death of a dream, and wondered if it was ever worth trying to build dreams at all.

He turned the bay pony around and headed back for the cabin. A quarter mile out, he saw the shape of an incoming rider and heeled the pony up to a gallop.

He came in with the Spencer canted over his saddle and sweat beading the horse's flanks. The rider was still some distance off, moving slowly, apparently unconcerned by Jubal's approach.

He turned the pony into the corral and ducked inside the cabin. Mary Wilson was preparing food and Jane Last was sitting with a life-size doll in her hands, slowly stroking the twists of yellow wool that formed the hair.

'What's yore hurry?' asked the old woman. 'Be a while before we eat.'

'Rider coming,' snapped Jubal. 'Coming slow, but he might be a decoy.'

Outside, the dog began to bark.

Mary Wilson set down the pan she was stirring and eased Jane onto her feet.

'Stir that, for me, honey.' She put the ladle into Jane's hands and moved away. 'Don't let it boil.'

Jane nodded and began to stir as the old woman hurried into the rear of the cabin. Jubal heard the shutters drop closed as he set the bars over the front windows.

The dog was still growling on the porch. He stroked the heavy neck and peered into the brightness. As the horse got closer he saw the outlines of a bulky figure, black vest unbuttoned over sweat-stained white shirt. A wide-brimmed stetson threw shadow over the face, but Jubal recognized Marshal Deke Tago from his size and lazy posture.

He cocked the Spencer.

The peace officer came in at a slow walk, guiding the horse with his left hand while his right mopped a kerchief over his florid face. If he saw the rifle Jubal was holding, he gave no sign. Just rode up to the porch and halted, sighing. Jubal waited. Behind him he could sense Mary Wilson. Inside the cabin he could hear Jane Last humming a tuneless song.

'Well?' Tago gave his face one last scrub and fumbled the kerchief into a vest pocket. 'You gonna invite me to climb down; or not?'

'Depends,' Jubal said cautiously, 'on if you're visiting or on official business.'

'Some of both, I guess,' shrugged Tago, wobbling his jowls. 'Was a long ride up here, though. Gives a man an appetite.'

Jubal nodded: 'Put your horse in the corral. Food's about ready.'

As the lawman climbed wearily down and took his pony round the house, Jubal turned to Mary Wilson.

'Get Jane into the bedroom. Fast!'

'What?' The old woman frowned. 'Poor child ain't eaten yet.'

'She's got a baby to tend,' rasped Jubal. 'Remember?'

'Christ! I damn' near forgot.'

She disappeared inside the cabin and the sounds of humming ceased as a door slammed shut. Deke Tago came onto the porch.

'You expectin' trouble?'

Jubal shrugged, easing the hammer of the Spencer down and cradling the rifle in his left arm.

'Thought you was leavin'?' The fat lawman paused, staring at Jubal. 'Thought we had us an agreement.'

'I was,' said Jubal. 'I got stopped by the Crazy Z.'

'Laz Stoppard's got a warrant sworn on you.' Tago hiked his thumbs under his belt, the movement shifting his gut. 'Claims you murdered two o' his boys. Cole Brandon an' a big feller called Eli. That right?'

'What d'you think?' Jubal asked.

Tago shrugged. 'I seen you in action, feller. I know you coulda done it. I'm askin' if you did.'

'How'd Stoppard tell the story?' Jubal demanded. 'Or did he write it for you, along with a persuader?'

The marshal chuckled. 'I guess you're tryin' to tell me you think Laz bought me out.' The grin faded and his face got weary. 'I ain't gonna deny I took money from Laz. Nor from Jason, either. I guess most folks know that. You know what I earn?'

Jubal shook his head.

'Fifty dollars a month,' said Tago. There was no more laughter in his voice. 'That's my wage. I get a room in back o' the jail if I want to sleep behind the drunks an' the horses. I buy my own cartridges an' I pay fer my own pony. When some cowboy downs too much whisky an' figgers to shoot up the town it's me has to go take the gun off him. Some owlhooter thinks to take the bank come payday, it's me faces him. I been a lawman fer close on thirty years an' I'm gettin' tired of bein' shot at an' spat on. I been hit three times. Spent four months in bed on account o' one bullet. An' I forgotten how many times I been beat up. Sure I take money from the ranchers. It's the only goddam way I know to stay alive long enough to retire. You want to tell me now?'

'I killed them,' said Jubal. 'Brandon stopped me on the north range. Took me in to the main ranch. Stoppard wanted me to sign a paper saying Gil Last disowned his son. Didn't want his wife to have the place. Stoppard thought that would give him a chance to buy the spread legally.'

Tago sighed and rubbed a hand over his face. 'I figgered it was somethin' like that. But you ain't explained about Cole an' Eli.'

'They beat me up.' Jubal indicated the marks on his face. 'I said I'd go along with Stoppard's plan, so they were taking me in to Gillard to sign the paper. I was going to leave them on the way. But Brandon woke up.'

'An' you killed them both.' Tago shook his head. 'Be hard to prove. Cole Brandon was mean an' fast. Eli was like a goddam grizzly. Be hard to prove a little feller like you killed 'em both in self defence.'

'You think I need to prove it?' Jubal asked.

'Laz swore out a warrant,' said Tago. 'It's my duty to take you back to stand trial. I don't like it, but I don't have no choice. I was hopin' you'd be gone. Like you said.'

'Stoppard fouled that up,' grunted Jubal. 'If it weren't for him I'd be long gone.'

'Wishin' ain't doin' it,' said Tago. 'You're here an' I'm here. Now I gotta take you in.'

'The hell you do!'

Mary Wilson's announcement was accompanied by the dull clicking of metal. The sound came from the twin hammers of the Remington scattergun she was holding on the lawman's belly. The twin muzzles were rock-hard on target.

Tago's fat face swung slowly round and sweat burst afresh over his porcine features.

'Christ Jesus!' His voice was suddenly hoarse. 'Put that thing down.'

'I known you too long, Deke Tago.' The shotgun didn't waver. 'I know how persuasive you are. An' how goddam sneaky. You put your guns down or I'll blow yore arse halfway home riderless.'

Tago went pale and reached over with his left hand to lift the Colt from his belt. He dropped it on the grass.

'Guns, I said,' snarled the old woman. 'All of 'em.'

Jubal watched as the marshal reached back behind his belt to tuck a cut-down Peacemaker from the back of his waist. Then his eyes got wide as a Remington derringer got pulled from the vest and a single-barrel, original Derringer came out from under the jacket.

'You watch him,' said Mary Wilson. 'He ain't half as slow as he looks. Nor so cuddly.'

'You're obstructing the course o' justice,' grunted Tago. 'I could arrest you fer haltin' an officer of the law in the course of his duty.'

'An' I could blow yore fat arse sideways into yore conscience, you fat-gut-no-good. But I won't. I'll feed yore face instead. We got sumthin' to tell you.'

Tago breathed a sigh of relief and followed the motion of the shotgun into the cabin. Jubal picked up his guns. Emptied them. And dropped them one by one on the porch.

Mary Wilson emptied the stew into a tureen and began to set places. The vegetables were already prepared, and the rich odours of good food filled the cabin. Jubal poured Deke Tago a cup of Gil Last's whisky and took one for himself.

'Where's Jane?' asked the lawman. 'Jason's askin' about her.'

'That's what we got to tell you.' The old woman scooped stew onto the plates. 'You listen to Jubal, now.'

'It better sound good,' rumbled Tago. 'So far you're both in a big mess o' trouble.'

Jubal began to talk as they ate.

'Jane's asleep in the bedroom,' he said. 'Her and the baby. I heard all about the will Gil Last made but after what's happened I don't reckon there's any court would stand by that. Way I see it, both Wain and Stoppard need this land. Trouble is, it belongs to Jane. If the Fat W tries to claim prior rights on account of the will, then they got a fight with the Cazy Z. If Stoppard tries to bullshit his plan through, he's got a war with Jason Wain. That make sense to you?'

Tago shrugged and wiped gravy off his face. 'I guess. In a twisted kinda way. Whatever one of 'em does, it leads to trouble.'

'And you're the law in Gillard,' said Jubal. 'You got jurisdiction over the county.'

'I'm responsible fer keepin' the peace,' admitted Tago, getting reluctant as he saw the implications of Jubal's argument. 'Yeah.'

'So if a range war starts,' grinned Jubal, 'you could be in trouble. At best you end up with one man in control. And no need to pay off for anyone else. At worst, you have a Federal Marshal come in.'

'Oh, Jesus!' Tago choked on the stew. 'I never thought of that.'

Mary Wilson chuckled. 'Best listen to the feller, Deke. He's got a real devious mind. Might even think up a way to fetch you outta trouble.'

'How?' Tago's plump face began to smile. 'You worked that out?'

'Maybe.' Jubal poured more whisky for the worried lawman. 'Depends on you.'

'Tell me.' Tago downed the drink in one. 'I'm gonna have some explainin' to do to Laz Stoppard if I don't bring you back. More fer Jase Wain.'

'Tell them both how Jane Last is back home,' said Jubal. 'Her and the baby. Tell them she's ready to talk on her own terms. She's deciding now if she wants to sell, or stay on. If she stays, the dams won't go up again so long as they both pay her water rights. If she decides to move out, then it's up to them to work an answer – so long as she gets a fair price.'

'Suppose they don't want to listen?' asked Tago. 'They ain't either of 'em gonna enjoy this.'

Jubal shrugged: 'You're in the middle now, Deke. Same as us. If a range war starts, then the Federals move in and you start explaining who's right and who's wrong enough to pay you money.'

'Shit!' Tago wiped his mouth. 'I was thinkin' to stay over. Now I reckon I'd best start back.'

'Yeah,' said Jubal. 'Fast.'

'What do I tell them?' asked the peace officer. 'Assuming they're ready to listen.'

'They come up here,' said Jubal. 'Together. No one with them except you and Henry Carter. Whatever gets agreed gets signed the same day.'

'An' you'll go?' asked Tago. 'You'll ride away an' not bother me no more.'

'Sure.' Jubal grinned. 'All I ever wanted was to get to Blazeville.'

Tago went out and fetched his horse from the corral. Jubal and Mary Wilson watched him ride away. The peace officer's shoulders were slumped even more than usual, but his pony was moving faster than on the way in.

'You think it'll work?' asked the old woman. 'It's a goddam long chance.'

'How come you swear so much?' Jubal countered.

'Shit!' she replied. 'I never thought I did. Besides, a goddam youngster like you don't have the right to ask a christly old lady personal questions.'

'No.' Jubal grinned. 'But sometimes asking questions people don't like is the only way to sort out a problem.'

'I don't understand,' she said. 'What in the goddam hell are you talkin' about?'

'Sometimes,' grunted Jubal, 'you get answers.'

## CHAPTER FOURTEEN

One full day passed before Tago returned. This time he was seated in a buckboard with a small, wiry-looking man beside him.

'Henry Carter,' he announced wearily. 'He ain't none too happy about your plan.'

Jubal studied the banker, trying to guess his character from his face. Carter was pushing sixty. His hair was grey, slicked down over a mottled pate with brilliantine that looked to have been applied in equal measure to the pointed moustache decorating his upper lip. His eyes matched the colour of his hair, and his face held the pallor of a man more accustomed to spending his days in a shaded office than riding buckboards over rough trails. Despite the heat, his brown suit was buttoned tight, and the bootlace spanning his stiff collar was drawn all the way up. He was sweating. And irritable.

'You'll be Cade,' he snapped. 'The author of this insane notion.'

'Step down.' Jubal held the Spencer loosely, ready to swing it on either man should they try anything. 'Have a drink.'

'Water.' Carter climbed from the buckboard. He was as short as he was thin. 'All I touch.'

'Henry's teetotal,' shrugged Tago. 'You got any of that whisky left?'

'Some.' Jubal moved back to flank the door. 'You drank most of it.'

'Figgered that.' Tago grinned. 'So I brought you a present. Figgered you might need some courage.'

'We'll go dutch.' Jubal caught the bottle the peace officer tossed him in his left hand, holding the Spencer with his right. On the marshal's chest.

Tago grunted and let his own hand slide gently clear of his holstered Colt.

'When you've finished playing games, Deke, perhaps we can get on with business.' Carter frowned, the puckering of lines making his face gnomish. 'The sooner we get this done, the better.'

'Sit an' drink yore water, Henry.' Mary Wilson came out from the cabin with the shotgun in her hands. 'Quit yore complainin'. Ain't nuthin' can be done afore Laz an' Jase get here.'

'They're on their way by now.' Carter made it sound menacing. 'I never thought to see you mixed up in a transaction like this, Mary.'

'I never been averse to a bit o' honest horse-tradin',' said the old woman. 'What I don't take to, is folks ganging up on a pore widder woman an' her child.'

'Ah, yes.' Carter stepped inside the cabin. 'The child. Where is the child? Since the baby is the ultimate legatee, I should like to see the infant.'

'In good time,' grunted Mary. 'Let's get Deke in here first.'

Jubal nodded and helped the marshal unhitch the team. They put the two horses in the corral and moved back towards the house.

'I saw two crosses,' murmured Tago; innocently. 'Who claims the second?'

'Gil Last,' Jubal said, his face bland. 'When we got back here, the first one was knocked down. Jane was upset, so I set another.'

Tago grunted some more and went into the cabin.

Henry Carter was sipping water with the daintiness of a St Louis lady. Jubal poured whisky for Tago and a smaller measure for himself.

'Well?' asked the banker. 'Do we see the widow and her child?'

'Sure.' Mary Wilson kept hold of the shotgun. 'But you gotta do it quietly. She had a hard time with the birth, an' now she's resting.'

She opened the door to the main bedroom, motioning them to silence.

The room was dark, the mid-day sun cut out by the shutters and the curtains. Jane Last was under the covers of the wide bed, her hair spread in a black fan over the pillows. Her eyes were closed in the sleep induced by a mixture of Mary Wilson's herbs and Jubal's morphine. Beside her, its woollen hair contrasting with the black, was the doll. It was wrapped in cloth: like swaddling robes. The woman's arms were around it, turning its cotton face to hers. In the dim light it looked as though the mother was holding her child.

'All right?' Mary Wilson eased the door shut. 'Now you seen it.'

'It was fair,' said Henry Carter. 'Both Jane and Gil Last had dark hair.'

'Christ!' The old woman shook her head. 'What colour's Jason's hair?'

'Blond,' Carter admitted. 'Very fair.'

'An' Jane's his daughter, ain't she?' The old woman sighed. 'Maybe the child resembles his grandfather.'

Both Carter and Tago appeared to accept the argument. They sat down at the table and began to nibble on the biscuits Mary had set out.

Neither man was at ease, and the air of tension inside the cabin mounted steadily as the sun climbed up to its zenith and the valley got filled with light.

The grass outside was mostly dried off now, the heat of the late summer evaporating the water spilled from the broken dams so that a thin mist rose shroud-like over the flat. It hung, ethereal, no more than a foot or two above the grass, cut through by the double lines of the streams and the natural heat of the cabin.

Jubal checked his watch: it was one hour after noon.

He began to ask when the two ranchers would arrive, but the sound of an approaching horse interrupted his words. He stepped out onto the porch and watched the rider coming in. Beside him, the big dog began to growl, the rasping sounds in its throat lifting to a savage bark as the horseman drew closer.

Jubal grabbed the animal by its collar and hauled it back inside the cabin. Mary Wilson took hold of it and kicked the door shut as the barking mounted to a steady baying. Deke Tago came out to stand alongside Jubal.

'Looks like Jason Wain,' he said. 'Don't know of anyone else rides a horse like that.'

Jubal peered through the deceptive alternation of flickering light. And saw what the fat lawman meant: the horse was taller by a hand, or more, than any he had seen. Its head was small, but beautifully shaped, a silvery grey mane complementing the dappled grey of the coat. It lifted its legs high as it cantered through the mist, almost prancing.

'Arab,' said Tago. 'He got it shipped in this year.'

Jubal nodded, studying the man.

He was tall, wearing a black shirt and matching pants. As he got closer, it was possible to pick out the silver threading over his breast. Two initials that read: JW. He wore a plain black belt around his waist, the holster carrying a long-barrelled Colt .45. He reined in close to the porch and stepped down without waiting to be asked. Swept off the wide, black stetson he wore to expose a thick mane of yellow hair, and said:

'Jason Wain. I know Deke, so you must be Jubal Cade.'

Jubal nodded.

'You killed two of my men.'

Wain hitched his horse to the porch.

'They forced it,' said Jubal. 'They didn't leave me much choice.'

'They don't matter,' said Wain. 'We'll not argue over that. Where's my daughter?'

It was hard to accept that he was around fifty years old. His body was lean and lithe, whipcord slender with the ease of movement that comes only from long hours of saddle work. His face was tanned and cleanly shaved, thin lines emanating from his eyes and mouth. The former were clear blue, set either side of a straight nose that would have assured his features of good looks had it not been for the mouth. That was wide and thin-lipped, as though carved on the face after birth. As though some godly knife had slashed a gap across his jaws so that he could speak.

'Inside,' said Jubal. 'Sleeping.'

'I want to see her.'

Jason Wain's voice held no doubt. There was no question in it: just the total assurance of a man accustomed to having his orders obeyed.

Jubal shrugged and stepped aside from the door. Deke Tago opened it.

Wain didn't thank him. Just stepped through and glanced around the cabin.

'She's asleep,' said Mary Wilson. 'I'll open the door so you can see her, but you ain't disturbin' her.'

Wain nodded, not bothering to reply.

He peered through the half-opened door and said, 'Why's she asleep? I thought she'd be awake for this.'

'She's sick,' answered the old woman. 'It was a hard birth.'

'I want to see the child,' said Wain. 'I want to see my grandson.'

Mary Wilson closed the door and said, 'Later. After Laz Stoppard gets here.'

Wain shrugged and sat down at the table. Without waiting for an invitation he poured himself a whisky. Tossed it off and poured a second.

'This won't work,' he said, looking at Jubal. 'I don't know what you think to get out of it, but it won't work.'

Jubal grinned and said, 'Nothing. All I want is to get out of here. To get to Blazeville.'

'Go now,' said Wain. 'Leave it to us to sort out. It's a family affair.'

'Other folks don't agree,' said Jubal, 'and I tried leaving once. Laz Stoppard's men held me up.'

'I heard about that.' Wain shrugged. 'I got pull with the authorities. I can get that charge dropped.'

'It's too late,' Jubal replied. 'I'm in too deep. Besides, someone has to look after your daughter.'

'I'll do that.' Wain's voice got cold and low, spitting from his thin lips like a snake's hiss. 'I don't need you to handle that.'

'She does,' rasped Jubal, the beginnings of anger flattening his own mouth to a narrow line. 'You've not done so well so far.'

'You're stupid.' Wain's voice was cold as ice. 'You've already bought off more trouble than you can handle. Ride away now. Leave it. I'll pay you a thousand to go.'

'Stoppard offered four,' said Jubal. 'To get my signature on paper.'

Wain glanced at Henry Carter and Deke Tago. They both nodded.

'All right,' he said. 'Five thousand. Six, if you'll quit right now.'

'How much is this place worth?' Jubal directed his question at the banker.

Henry Carter furrowed his narrow lids and began to make mental sums. Mary Wilson speeded them with a nudge from the twin muzzles of the shotgun.

'Hard to say.' Carter got worried, plucking at his string tie so that it came loose from his collar. 'Given the site. Given that Gil bought it fair, I'd say around twenty-five thousand on current prices.'

'Can you afford that?' Jubal asked. 'That much?'

Jason Wain shook his head: 'No. But I can take it.'

'Now hold on, Jase.' Deke Tago came into the conversation. 'You start talkin' like that, an' you're talkin' about range wars an' Federal Marshals. There's none of us want that. Right, Henry?'

The banker shook his head. 'He's right, Mister Wain. I hate to say it, but Cade makes sense. If you – or Mister Stoppard – try to take over this place illegally, then both the marshal's superiors and my own will begin an investigation. That could tie the land up in Federal hands for months. Years, even. And whoever began the war would lose out.'

'Shit!' snarled Wain, losing his cultured accent. 'So I gotta sit on my arse an' listen to this goddam late-comer.'

'I think so,' said Carter. 'I really do think so.'

Wain looked at the marshal, his blue eyes framing a question. 'How come you don't just arrest him, Deke? If Stoppard posted a warrant on him, can't you take him in?'

'Still mean the Federal people, Jase.' Tago shrugged, his jowls trembling as he felt himself caught between two opposing forces. 'Way I see it, you hafta go along with Cade's plan.'

'You're finished,' snarled Wain. 'Both of you.'

On the porch, the dog began to bark.

Jubal stood up, lifting the Spencer.

'See who it is,' said Mary Wilson, angling the scattergun on the men seated around the table. 'I'll keep these fellers quiet.'

'Thanks.'

Jubal stepped onto the porch and watched Laz Stoppard ride in.

'Gonna see you dead,' said the rancher. 'Cole an' Eli were good boys.'

'Not good enough,' said Jubal. 'Not quite good enough.'

'I'll still see you hang,' said Stoppard. 'Or gunned down.'

Jubal grinned. 'Before that, you got some dealing to do. You and Wain. With Carter and Tago as witnesses.'

Stoppard's scarred face broke into an ugly smile. 'You're dead, feller. You don't ever leave this valley alive.'

Jubal shrugged, and asked: 'What's Laz stand for?'

'Lazarus.' Stoppard dismounted, irritated by the question. 'Why?'

'I just wondered,' said Jubal, pushing the boss of the Crazy Z into the cabin. 'But I thought it might.'

'How come?' Stoppard halted in the doorway. 'What the goddam hell you talkin' about?'

'You keep rising to the bait,' said Jubal.

And shoved the rancher in through the door.

## CHAPTER FIFTEEN

'It make sense.'

Henry Carter swallowed his ninth glass of water and tugged the stud of his wing collar loose from his neck.

'It has to make sense: it's the only way.'

'The hell it does.' Laz Stoppard emptied a glass of whisky and glowered at Jason Wain. 'Soon as that child comes of age, the land goes to him.'

Wain just grinned. Complacently.

'Suppose there wasn't a baby?' Jubal said. 'What then?'

Silence fell on the darkening cabin. Henry Carter stopped tugging at his collar and Deke Tago set down his glass. Jason Wain stared at Jubal through eyes like chips of blue ice. Laz Stoppard twisted round in his seat and set one hand over the butt of the gun holstered on his left side.

'What the goddam hell you talkin' about?' He spoke for all of them. 'This another of yore games?'

Jubal nodded to Mary Wilson, who backed out of the room to fetch Jane Last from the bedroom.

The widow still clutched the big doll, stroking its woollen hair and clutching the painted face against her own bleak pallor.

'The baby died,' said Jubal. 'Now you have to sort things out with the widow.'

'The hell we do!'

Laz Stoppard's gun was halfway clear of the holster before he heard the ugly click of the scattergun's hammers going back.

'You work out a deal,' said Jubal. 'You do it now. In front of witnesses.'

He set paper and pencils before both men as the Colt sank slowly back into Stoppard's holster.

'What do you want, Jane?'

'I want to go away from here.' Her voice was dull with grief, barely audible. She went on cradling the toy. 'I want my child to grow up someplace nice. Not like I did.'

'She's mad,' said Wain. 'That's right, ain't it, Carter?'

The banker nodded. 'It seems that way, Mister Wain.'

'So I get the land as next of kin.'

'No, Daddy.' Jane Last's voice echoed clear through the cabin. 'I don't want you to have it. Me and Gil built this place, but you did nothing but hurt us. I don't want you owning what we built.'

'I'll buy it,' said Laz Stoppard. 'Henry here said it was worth maybe twenty-five thousand. I'll pay that right now. Henry can authorize the note.'

'Twenty-five thousand?' Her voice sounded dull; disinterested by the enormous sum. 'That should take care of my baby.'

'For Godsake!' Wain argued. 'That crazy bitch can't be held responsible for what she's doing.'

'She can sign papers,' said Stoppard. 'You lost it, Wain.'

'Well?' Jubal asked. 'Can she sign paper, or not?'

'I think so,' said Carter. 'She seems reasonable enough, except for this thing about the baby.'

'This?' asked Jane. 'This toy?'

She dropped the doll. It fell to the floor. She put a foot on the painted face and ground her heel down into the sacking so that it split apart at the seams, bleeding sawdust like dusty blood over the floor. She kicked it across the room and turned, smiling, to face the startled eyes around the table.

'You stupid bastards!' Colour filled her cheeks and her eyes blazed. 'You think you can buy me off that easy? You think I don't know what this place is worth? You think Gil didn't explain it to me?'

'Jane! Jane, honey.' Mary Wilson stepped up, to the younger woman, arms spread wide. 'You're hurt. You're upset.'

'The goddam hell I am!'

Jane Last pushed the old woman aside and picked up the scattergun. Mary Wilson fell down with a gasp of surprise. She sprawled on the floor, skirts hiked up to expose scarlet bloomers, her mouth gaping open, threatening to spill her false teeth loose.

'You miserable old bitch!' Jane's eyes took fire as she swung the scattergun around the room. 'All you ever did was tell me how bad men were. How bad my father was! How bad Gil was! Jesus! He was bad enough, but he was better than listening to you. He took me out of it, at least. More'n my dear daddy ever did. But you! All you did was tell me how bad everyone was. Now you can see.'

She shoved the scattergun into Mary Wilson's mouth and squeezed a trigger.

The heavy gauge shot exploded from the right-hand barrel in a pattern that would have spread into a diamond shape had it not been contained by the configurations of the old woman's skull. Instead, the main force of the blast was directed against the floor. Mary Wilson's head banged back as the boards bucked under the discharge. Pellets bounced off teeth and bones to emerge from her cheeks. The false teeth exploded upwards, blown out by the hideously imploded detonation. They came out on the upward fountaining of a long column of blood, and snapped once on Jane Last's dress before clattering to the floor. The old woman's flesh was shredded by the blast, the loose skin between cheekbones and jaws ripped apart so that bare bones and bleeding gums showed clear through the holes.

Jane turned, lifting the scattergun towards the table.

Jubal powered sideways as he saw the second barrel swing in his direction.

'Daddy!' Jane Last screamed. 'You killed my baby.'

She fired the second barrel as Jason Wain stood up.

'I never mattered more to you than my momma did!'

Wain's face got shredded while he was still saying, 'No. It wasn't me.'

From Jubal's position on the floor it was like seeing a skull stripped of its flesh. The teeth crumpled back into the jaw as the eyes disappeared into the gaping holes of the skull sockets. The nose gouted a column of blood as it was mangled back into the bone behind. The tanned flesh tore clear of the broken structure beneath, fluttering like tattered pennants of lost life in the wind of the pellets' passing. The blond hair became abruptly red, the outcharge of blood from the ravaged skull colouring it with the shades of death.

Jason Wain screamed and fell back against the wall of the cabin.

Where he fell, he left a massive swathe of blood that gouted down the planking in thick globules of crimson, interlaced with the whiter fragments of skin and the grey lumps of brain matter.

Laz Stoppard drew his Colt and angled the revolver on Jane Last.

He was pulling the trigger as Jubal turned the Spencer in his direction and shouted, 'No!'

It was too late.

The triple click of the Colt's hammer got drowned under its discharge. Flame spurted from the muzzle, accompanied by a cloud of black powder smoke.

Jane Last screamed like her father as the bullet took her through the lower ribs. It punched in through her belly, doubling her over as her arms stretched out and her hands spread wide to release the scattergun that fell with an empty clatter onto the floor. It went on through her heart, tearing the vital organ into shreds before ricocheting off a hindward rib to emerge from her back.

She was slammed against the stove, her body arcing as a thin trickle of blood fell from her mouth. The coffee pot got overturned and the stench of cordite was abruptly overlayed with the sharper reek of burning hair.

Flames started up around her face, and the blood coming from her mouth and back began to sizzle.

Jubal squeezed the trigger of the Spencer without thinking.

Knowing only anger. His face was contorted into a mask of rage that spread his lips into a thin line and tugged the skin across his cheekbones taut, so that the line of white scar tissue over his nose stood out against the tan.

In that moment of total rage he could not know whether he fired the rifle for his own sake, or for Jane Last, or for Mary Wilson. The fury possessed him and he knew no more than that. Could not know any more: only that he needed to kill. Wanted to kill. And that all his hate was now directed at Laz Stoppard.

The rancher's body jerked under the impact, spinning clear of the blood-stained table as the .30 calibre slug bit deep into the ribs. The bullet entered low on the right side, shattering a rib before ploughing upwards into the lung. Stoppard screamed and twisted sideways, collapsing over a chair that overturned to spill his body onto the floor.

Jubal levered the Spencer and fired again as the body came down. His second shot glanced off Stoppard's belt buckle, ricocheting upwards into the man's face so that it tore in under his jaw and punched a hole through the roof of his mouth into the pan of his brain. It mangled the soft material hidden inside his skull and lodged against the upper bone, splitting it slightly, so that a thin trickle of blood and oozing matter spilled through his hair.

The body hit the floor with its legs tangled in the chair and the mouth wide open. From both corners of the lips there merged a thick pulsing of crimson that was flecked through with bubbles. The twin trickles ran down over the jaws and began to drip onto the floor, joining the mess that was already spreading from Jason Wain's ruined face and Mary Wilson's shattered skull.

Jane Last's body dropped from the stove, the burning of her hair filling the cabin with the acrid stink of dying.

Henry Carter began to retch. Jubal stood up, turning the rifle on Deke Tago.

The marshal climbed to his feet with both hands in the air.

'I got no quarrel with you, feller. I just come along as a witness.'

'So you watched it all,' grated Jubal. 'All fair.'

'Sure.' Tago nodded enthusiastically. 'Ain't nuthin' to charge you with. Ain't that right, Henry?'

Carter pressed a handkerchief to his mouth and nodded as he ran for the door.

'Whatever you say, Deke. Sure.'

There was the sound of vomiting, and the dog barking. Jubal realized it had been barking since the shooting began: he just hadn't heard it.

'Now what?' he asked. 'Who claims the place now?'

Tago glanced around the smoke-filled room. Mary Wilson was stretched on the floor with most of her head missing. Jane Last was still bleeding, her hair smouldering as blood and fire met. Jason Wain and Laz Stoppard were sprawled together, their blood mingling in death as their ambitions had never done in life.

'No one, I guess,' said the lawman. 'Henry'll send word to the next of kin when he's finished spewin', and I'll let the Federal people know what happened. I'll tell the hands from the Fat W an' the Crazy Z their bosses killed one another. Reckon Henry'll go along with that.'

He shrugged, grinning at Jubal.

'Shit! It's gonna save Gillard a range war.'

'That's right,' grunted Jubal. 'That's what Mary Wilson wanted.'

'What about her?' asked Tago. 'Come to that, what about all of 'em?'

'How'd you mean?' Jubal asked. 'I don't understand.'

'Yeah.' Tago spat. 'You're a doctor – you just heal 'em. Me, I'm a marshal. I hafta bury them.'

Jubal shrugged and opened the stove. He went into the bedrooms and tossed the kerosene lanterns over the beds, then came back into the main room and smashed the two lamps there on the floor.

Tago backed out the door as Jubal said, 'Easy.'

And struck a match, tossing the flame into the centre of the widening pool of kerosene.

The inflammable liquid burst into ravaging life. It spread over the floor, taking hold on the rugs and the bodies. Smoke began to spill through the closed shutters as the curtains took flame, and the dog began to bark, snapping at the tendrils of smoke that burst through the door.

'Yeah, I guess that's the best way,' said Tago. 'What you think, Henry?'

The banker looked up and took a breath of the smoke. He began to gag again.

'Henry agrees,' said the peace officer. And chuckled. 'It's funny, but I'm kinda glad to be rid o' them two. Ole Jase was waxin' a might too big.'

'And Laz,' said Jubal, 'won't rise again.'

# CHAPTER SIXTEEN

Tago and Carter fetched the two wagons from the corral while Jubal led the saddle mounts clear of the blaze. The dog pranced around his heels, alternately whining and barking at the conflagration. The fire, contained within the shuttered cabin, took hold fast, sending off waves of heat that set the air to shimmering, mirage-like. Tongues of flame licked through the joins of shutters and door like beckoning fingers, and from the chimney there spurted a single column of fire.

After a while part of the roof fell in, gusting a great cloud of sparks and black smoke into the sky. The three men stood in silence, shading their faces from the heat as they watched the funeral pyre. Like mourners. The door burned away, and the cabin seemed to emit a tired sigh that thrust heat and fire out over the grass beyond, singeing it and covering the little vegetable garden with a layer of dark ash. A corner post gave way, spilling one wall down in a rain of dancing sparks through which it was just possible to make out the bodies. Cartridges exploded in the gunbelts of the two ranchers, the detonations almost lost under the roaring of the main blaze. More of the roof collapsed, hiding the corpses and filling the late afternoon sky with red and gold flame. A tall column of roiling smoke lifted up like a beacon through the still air, setting a black exclamation mark against the clear blue.

Tago was the first to speak.

'Why'd she do that?'

'Who?' Jubal watched a second wall go down. 'Who d'you mean?'

'Jane,' said the lawman, quietly. 'Why'd she kill Mary? The old biddy never done nuthin' but help the girl.'

'I don't know,' murmured Jubal. 'She was mixed up with

grief. She lost her husband and her child. Maybe she blamed Mary.'

'She was clearly insane.' Henry Carter wiped a handkerchief over his vomit-stained moustache. 'Out of her mind. I'd never have countenanced her signature on those spurious documents.'

'Christ!' Tago grunted, still staring at the blaze. 'Why don't you shut yore mouth, Henry? The pore kid's dead an' gone. Have some respect.'

Carter frowned, shaking his kerchief with a look of distaste on his thin face. 'I still have the paper work to handle, Deke.'

'You an' me both,' said the peace officer. 'But I gotta explain this to the cowboys.'

The cabin groaned, thrusting thick fingers of flame from all its angles. The bricks of the chimney glowed red in the sunlight, and smoke tumbled in oily waves from the gaps in the walls. Then there was a dull reverberation, like thunder echoing from faraway hills, and the entire structure collapsed in on itself.

For a moment there was only a blinding flash of flame and a solid wave of heat. Jubal felt his hair scorch and then his nostrils were filled with the stink of burning, watering his eyes and prompting him to turn away.

When he looked back, blinking to clear his vision, the cabin was gone. In its place was a mound of smouldering timber, only the chimney still standing upright. The bodies – or what still remained of them – were lost beneath the debris, and the main force of the blaze died down to a steady burning that sent a tall, unwavering line of smoke into the sky.

Jubal became aware of the dog beside him. The animal was crouched on its hindquarters, jaws gaping wide and dark eyes fixed on the ruins. It threw back its head and let loose a single wailing cry. Then it tucked its tail between its legs and stared at Jubal.

'What you gonna do about him?' asked Tago.

Jubal shrugged, scratching the big dog's head. 'I can't take him with me.'

The marshal began to draw his Colt, but Jubal said, 'No! Don't kill him. Take him back to town. Maybe someone'll give him a home.'

'He eats too much,' said Tago. 'Besides, that thing's a one-man animal, an' it looks like he picked you.'

Jubal reached inside his coat, pulling out the wad of notes Joe Farmer and Norm Clayton had tried to steal. He peeled off fifty dollars and handed them to the lawman.

'That should look after him for a while. Take him back with you.'

Tago shrugged. 'You're crazy, but all right; I'll do it.'

'Thanks.' Jubal led the dog over to Mary Wilson's wagon and hitched a rope from the tail-board to the dog's collar. 'Thanks a lot.'

'Don't thank me,' grunted Tago. 'Just get the hell outta here. I hope we don't meet again.'

Jubal grinned, ducking his head in agreement. He swung astride the bay pony and turned north. The day was getting late, but he thought he could make the far end of the valley and get up onto the ridge before the light went. Sleep over in the timber, and then move on to Blazeville the next day.

He rode out past the wreckage of the northern dam and began to climb the slope as the light faded from the valley. It was still bright along the rimrock, and where the valley split into its southern fold, he could just make out the shapes of the two wagons heading back to Gillard. The cabin was still burning, filling the centre of the valley with a dull red glow, like metal heated in a forge. Or dreams burning out.

He picked his way up through the pines slowly, wary of cowboys coming in to check the blaze. Off to the east, the sky was dark, black at the horizon but striated from there into bands of colour that shaded from blue to green to silver that was tinged with the colour of blood and gold where the sun was going down in the west. Up on the rimrock the air was cool, and the big pines covered the ground with shadow. An owl hooted somewhere above him and a bird he couldn't recognize chattered angrily in reply.

He topped the rim and headed north through the dying light. The sun was hidden now behind the western ranges, succeeding only in spilling a red glow across the topmost hills. He found a hollow that was ringed with old conifers, the walls bare rock cut through with roots. The bottom was grassed over, so he hobbled the bay pony and left it cropping the grass as he prepared a fire. He cooked the food he had taken from Mary Wilson's wagon and brewed coffee, thinking about the cabin and Jane Last and Mary Wilson.

He wished he had brought some whisky with him.

In the morning he just drank coffee, then saddled the bay pony and moved on in the direction of Blazeville.

It was soon after dawn and the birds were scarcely started on their chorus. The air was cool, the mist just getting cleared by the rising sun so that the rimrock was shifting between shadow and light and greyness. Very still; absent of movement.

The shot surprised him, for he had allowed the events of the previous day and the quietness of the morning to dull his senses. He cursed himself as it rang through the trees and set the bay pony to bucking, threatening to pitch him from the saddle onto the rocks surrounding the trail.

Then inbred habit took control and he hiked his feet loose from the stirrups and allowed his body to tumble clear of the horse. He struck the side of the trail with the Spencer in his right hand. As he landed against a thrust of roots he levered the rifle and slapped his left hand around the barrel.

Sliding down the outspill of the big pine he turned the Spencer towards where he thought the muzzle-flash had come from. Triggered a shot.

It sang loose through the timber.

The bay pony careened up the path.

A second shot drove it around a bend in the trail.

A third plucked dirt from the earth above Jubal's head as he looked for the siting of the second.

He was levering the Spencer for another chance when the voice rang out: a voice he recognized.

'I got you dead. Drop the rifle.'

The statement was emphasized by a fourth bullet that twisted his derby sideways off his head, ploughing into the bank behind his position so that dirt splattered over his face.

He dropped the rifle.

And the gunman he had met before came down the far bank.

The man was devoid of his coat now, so that Jubal saw him more clearly. He wore a black hat with a silver band around the crown; a dirty white shirt and black pants that were studded with silver conchos that matched the decorations on his gunbelt and holster. The holster was filled with a Colt .45 Frontier model. His hands were filled with a Winchester carbine in .44.–40 calibre.

He still wore the odd waistcoat, all banded through with silvery threads. Like some kind of wire stitching. It shone in the early light.

'Stand up.'

Jubal climbed to his feet.

'They're all dead,' said the man. 'Aren't they?'

'Who?' Jubal eased out to the centre of the trail, where a ricochet wouldn't hit him. 'Who are you talking about?'

'Jason Wain an' the others. Jane Last. The people in the cabin.'

'Yeah,' said Jubal. 'Why?'

'You don't know? They never told you?'

Jubal shook his head.

The gunman chuckled. 'Maybe they never knew. I thought they would. Pity, because now I have to kill you.'

'Why?' Jubal asked again. 'I don't even know who you are.'

'Name's Wain,' said the gunman. 'Nathan Wain. Jane was my sister, except the old man never knew that. He just spread his seed around an' rode on. Only kin he ever went back to find was Jane. That was why he let her marry that cowboy an' then looked after her.'

'He didn't,' said Jubal. 'He hated Gil Last. He tried to drive him off.'

'Don't kid me.' Nathan Wain sneered, his face getting ugly. 'Only one tried to drive them off was Stoppard. Old Father Wain let 'em stay there.'

'That why you killed on both sides?' asked Jubal, taking a guess. 'That why you killed Gil Last?'

Wain laughed. 'Sure. Why the hell should that no-good bastard marry my sister an' set himself up so nice? I wanted to kill him, anyway. Fixing the range war was somethin' else.'

'You could've introduced yourself,' said Jubal, 'to your father. He might have welcomed a son.'

'No.' Nathan shook his head. 'He left my momma to fend for herself. He never even knew I was alive.'

'He'll never know now,' said Jubal. 'He's dead.'

'Yeah,' said Nathan. 'That's why I have to kill you.'

'Why?' Jubal asked. 'I only came into this by accident. All I want is to get to Blazeville.'

'Because you fouled my plans,' snarled Nathan. 'I shot Gil Last so I could claim that spread. Saving the baby spoiled all that.'

Jubal began to chuckle and the gunman frowned, beginning to ask him why until a loud barking interrupted his question.

'They got dogs?' he asked. 'They send dogs after me?'

'No.' Jubal shook his head. 'No dogs, no baby. Jane lost the child. She went crazy at the end. Shot her father and got killed herself.'

'Might be that we're all a little crazy,' said Nathan. 'My momma was.'

'You said it,' said Jubal, 'not me.'

The barking died away and the rimrock got silent except for the birdsong and the chattering of squirrels. A wind had got started up from the north, blowing down through the trees so that the branches waved and whistled softly in the early light.

'I have to kill you,' said Nathan Wain. 'It's just got to be done. I told you to leave once, but you ignored me. Now I have to do it.'

He lowered the hammer onto the breech of the Winchester and set the carbine aside.

'I give everyone a chance: I never draw first.'

The wind went on blowing through the trees as Jubal stared at the gunman. He wondered if there was a strain of madness running through the Wain blood. Jason had announced his own daughter insane, and Jane had lived up to that condemnation. Nathan appeared tainted by the same derangement.

Jubal stripped his jacket off and said, 'It doesn't have to be like this. There's no need for us to fight.'

'You killed my sister,' snarled Nathan. 'If it weren't for you I'd be owning that place now.'

'You're crazy,' said Jubal, listening to the wind and the other sounds that came slowly from the trees. 'You got no fight with me.'

'You draw first,' repeated Nathan. 'I always give a man a chance.'

Jubal swung his coat round and powered to the side. He couldn't tell if it was sixth sense or certainty that told him Nathan Wain's silver threaded vest was a bullet-proof mesh of steel and padded cloth. He only knew that he was worried by the man's confidence, and his insistence that Jubal draw first.

He threw the jacket into Wain's face and triggered a shot at the gunman's belly.

It hit where the vest joined. Wain staggered back, swiping the coat clear of his face as he drew his own gun and fired at Jubal.

The smaller man was rolling aside, fetching up against the edge of the trail ten feet clear of Nathan's position.

Wain laughed and fanned two shots in Jubal's direction. The wild motion spun the bullets feet wide of Jubal, who fired again, aiming his bullet at the belly.

Wain went on laughing as the slugs bounced off his vest. He was bounced back against the side of the trail, stumbling away as Jubal fired with the precision of habit at his belly and chest.

He rolled clear as Jubal's gun emptied and the hammer clicked on empty cylinders.

'Like I told you,' he grinned. 'I always give the other man a chance.'

Jubal snapped the loading gate of his Colt open. The Spencer was too far away to risk. He began to thumb the ejector rod, pumping the spent shells clear.

Nathan Wain laughed and cocked his pistol as he stepped out into the centre of the trail.

'I gave you a chance,' he laughed, voice lifting to a high-pitched shriek. 'An' you lost it.'

The Colt clicked loud in the sudden silence.

And then a fury of sound burst from the trees flanking the path. It began as a low-pitched growling. Lifted up to a bloodthirsty baying, and mounted to a guttural scream as the dog launched itself at Nathan Wain.

The gunman twisted round as the big dog came out from the rise flanking the path. He turned his gun and triggered one shot that burned hair from the animal's ribs. Then screamed as the massive body struck him and carried him down. He went on screaming as the jaws fastened on his neck, yellow teeth biting deep into his throat, severing the windpipe as the fangs tore through flesh and cartilage to emerge with a bloody mouthful of dripping, pulpy skin and pipes.

The dog jammed its paws against Wain's shoulders. Began to scrabble its hind paws against his stomach.

And went on tearing chunks of flesh out of his throat even after he fired the Colt into its belly so that spraying fountains of blood gouted from the animal's back, the force of the bullet lifting its body clear.

Jubal finished loading his Colt and ran over to the two bodies.

The big dog was on its side. There was a hole in the belly and a much larger one just in front of the hindquarters. It was panting, still snapping its teeth against the pieces of Nathan Wain's throat. The grey hair was covered with blood.

Jubal sighed. And levelled the Colt against the dog's skull.

The dark eyes stared at him, open and friendly. Hurting.

He stroked the big head and squeezed the trigger.

The skull exploded into happiness and Jubal turned to Nathan Wain.

The man was on his back, both hands pressed tight against the hole that had been his throat. Blood pulsed from between his clutching fingers, trickling out over his metal vest. It ran down over his chest, staining the silvery threading and the conchos on his pants.

'I could've had it all,' he gargled. 'All of it.'

'No,' said Jubal. 'That was the last place you'd have had.'

He lifted the Colt and pushed the barrel in between Nathan Wain's teeth. Squeezed the trigger.

And watched as the head exploded into fragments of bone-flecked blood.

Then he went to find the bay pony and Wain's horse. Hitched them together and set out along the road to Blazeville.

He left the bodies on the trail, the dog and the man linked together in death. Behind him, the cabin still smouldered: a memory of revenge and madness and mistake.

When he finally reached Blazeville he sold Nathan's horse and went looking for Lee Kincaid. The outlaw band was broken up, its members shot or driven off, but no one could confirm that the scar-faced man had been amongst the survivors. What was certain was that he did not number amongst the dead. A few members of the posse claimed to recognize one of the outlaws from Jubal's description, but none could say what had happened to him or where he might have gonc.

In a way, Jubal was glad: he wanted Kincaid for himself. It was a dream, perhaps as wild as the dream that had killed Gil Last, but it was still the purpose of his wandering, the thing that drove him on.

After a few days he left Blazeville. He had no special destination, just the single, burning purpose. And the determination to fulfil his own dream.

**THE BEST IN WESTERNS FROM GRANADA PAPERBACKS**

**Matt Chisholm**

| | |
|---|---|
| Kill McAllister | 50p ☐ |
| McAllister: Tough to Kill | 50p ☐ |
| McAllister Rides | 50p ☐ |
| McAllister Strikes | 40p ☐ |
| McAllister: Hell for McAllister | 40p ☐ |
| McAllister: The Hard Men | 40p ☐ |
| Kiowa | 40p ☐ |
| McAllister Justice | 40p ☐ |
| McAllister: The Hangman Rides Tall | 40p ☐ |
| McAllister: Death at Noon | 40p ☐ |
| Hell for McAllister | 40p ☐ |
| McAllister | 40p ☐ |

**Charles R Pike**

| | |
|---|---|
| Jubal Cade 1: The Killing Trail | 60p ☐ |
| Jubal Cade 2: Double Cross | 60p ☐ |
| Jubal Cade 3: The Hungry Gun | 60p ☐ |
| Jubal Cade 4: Killer Silver | 60p ☐ |
| Jubal Cade 5: Vengeance Hunt | 60p ☐ |
| Jubal Cade 6: The Burning Man | 60p ☐ |
| Jubal Cade 7: The Golden Dead | 60p ☐ |
| Jubal Cade 8: Death Wears Grey | 60p ☐ |
| Jubal Cade 9: Days of Blood | 60p ☐ |
| Jubal Cade 10: The Killing Ground | 50p ☐ |
| Jubal Cade 11: Brand of Vengeance | 65p ☐ |
| Jubal Cade 12: Bounty Road | 65p ☐ |

**WAR FICTION – AVAILABLE IN GRANADA PAPERBACKS**

**W A Ballinger**
Women's Battalion 75p ☐

**H E Bates**
The Stories of Flying Officer X 65p ☐

**William D Blankenship**
Tiger Ten 75p ☐

**Harry Brown**
A Walk in the Sun 70p ☐

**C S Forester**
Brown on Resolution 60p ☐
Death to the French 60p ☐

**Alexander Fullerton**
A Wren Called Smith 40p ☐
The Waiting Game 95p ☐

**John Oliver Killens**
And Then We Heard the Thunder 95p ☐

**Guy Kingston**
Main Force 85p ☐

**Hans Helmut Kirst**
The Lieutenant Must Be Mad 40p ☐

*All these books are available at your local bookshop or newsagent, or can be ordered direct from the publisher. Just tick the titles you want and fill in the form below.*

---

Name ..................................................

Address ..................................................

..................................................

Write to Granada Cash Sales, PO Box 11, Falmouth, Cornwall TR10 9EN.

Please enclose remittance to the value of the cover price plus:

UK: 30p for the first book, 15p for the second book plus 12p per copy for each additional book ordered to a maximum charge of £1.29.

BFPO and EIRE: 30p for the first book, 15p for the second book plus 12p per copy for the next 7 books, thereafter 6p per book.

OVERSEAS: 50p for the first book and 15p for each additional book.

*Granada Publishing reserve the right to show new retail prices on covers, which may differ from those previously advertised in the text or elsewhere.*